REWIND BOOK TWO

An Adventure in Time Travel,
(a Journey to Déjà Vu!)

Copyright 2025

Join us on Facebook
scan QR code below

Website
https://www.facebook.com/rewindtimetravelbookseries

SYNOPSIS

*The beginning of book two
introduces the second main
character of the time travel series.
Jacob Walker is an 18-year-old
son of a local beekeeper located
in the town of Mineral Springs.
His family sends him on a trip
to New York City to attend his
great uncle's funeral, and witness
the reading of the will. On his
trip to New York City, he gets
ready to take his first subway
ride. Unknown to Jacob, Mason
Anderson is also in New York, he
has found the time travel device,
and is currently running from Nasa
agents. Nasa has discovered the
unknown secret that the device*

can travel to a specific time in history, which they want to use to alter history. Mason doesn't want Nasa to use his device in such a way so he takes the device and is running from Nasa. Book two covers their trip, and events which leads to them joining forces and take them on their next time travel adventure in book three.

Dedication

To my adventurous spirit, the one who always dared to leap before looking, who embraced the unexpected detours and celebrated the unplanned journeys. This story is a testament to the power of those unplanned adventures, to the serendipitous encounters and the unforeseen consequences that shape us. It's a tribute to the belief that even in the midst of chaos, even when confronted with the seemingly impossible, a little bit of hope, a dash of humor, and a whole lot of heart can lead to extraordinary discoveries. It's a nod to those who find magic in the mundane, who see the extraordinary potential in the everyday. For those who find themselves
unexpectedly flung through time, and for those who patiently wait for them on the other side of the temporal divide, this book is dedicated to you.

To my family, whose unwavering support, patience, and belief in me have fueled my creative fire through countless late nights, countless revisions, and countless cups of coffee. You have been my anchors amidst the storms of writer's block, my cheerleaders when doubt crept in, and my constant source of inspiration. This book is a culmination of all the stories we've shared, all the laughter we've exchanged, and all the love that binds us together. You are the real-life time travelers, traversing the unpredictable landscape of life with me, and I am eternally grateful. Thank you for believing in my impossible dreams, even when they seemed just as outlandish as a time-traveling device hidden in a subway briefcase.

To my friends, the fellow adventurers, the fellow storytellers, the fellow dreamers. Those who understand the peculiar magic of words, the boundless possibilities of imagination, and the
unwavering necessity of sharing stories. Your camaraderie, your encouragement, and your willingness to engage in endless
discussions about character arcs, plot twists, and the ultimate

meaning of life (or the lack thereof) have made this journey incredibly rich and incredibly fun. Thank you for being the constant reminder that the best adventures are shared, the best stories are collaboratively created, and the best companions are the ones who journey alongside you, even if you're both tumbling through time and the Great Depression.

To the curious souls who stumble upon these pages, seeking a little escape, a little adventure, a little laughter, and a little bit of heart in the whirlwind that is life. May the stories within these pages

transport you, inspire you, and remind you that even the most ordinary of lives can hold extraordinary adventures. May you

always embrace the unknown, chase your impossible dreams, and never stop believing in the power of a good story – or a well-timed two-hundred-dollar donation. Because let's face it, sometimes even a small act of kindness can reverberate through time, leaving an impact far greater than we could ever imagine.

Unexpected Encounter

The air hung thick and humid in the already stifling New York City subway car. Jacob Walker, clutching a crumpled tissue in his sweaty palm, felt a familiar knot of anxiety tighten in his stomach. His great-uncle Silas's funeral loomed large, a somber event he'd rather avoid, but family obligations, however grim, were not easily ignored. The metallic scent of the train, a pungent mix of sweat, exhaust fumes, and something vaguely chemical, filled his nostrils. He shifted uncomfortably, the worn fabric of his seat offering little comfort against the relentless jostling of the packed carriage. Each screech of the brakes sent a fresh wave of unease through him; he'd never been a fan of the subway, a fact his urban-dwelling cousins found endlessly amusing.

He squeezed his eyes shut for a moment, trying to conjure the image of his great-uncle, a man he barely knew but who, according to family lore, had lived a life both fascinating and mysterious. Silas, the eccentric inventor, the solitary recluse, the man who'd amassed a fortune through some unspecified means and died leaving behind a legacy of both intrigue and unanswered questions. The will reading, scheduled for later that day, hung over Jacob like a dark cloud, promising revelations he wasn't entirely prepared to face.

When he opened his eyes, he found himself staring at his unexpected seatmate: a man who looked as though he'd just escaped from a particularly chaotic scene. Mason Anderson, as the worn leather briefcase resting on his knees proclaimed in faded gold lettering, seemed to be practically vibrating with a nervous energy that was almost palpable. He was thin, almost gaunt, with eyes that darted around the carriage like trapped birds. His hands, long and restless, fidgeted with the clasp of the briefcase, occasionally reaching inside to touch something unseen. The man's clothes, while clean, were rumpled and slightly too large, giving him a perpetually rumpled appearance, as if he'd been hastily dressed and was constantly on the verge of flight. A faint, almost imperceptible tremor ran through his entire body.

Jacob watched, fascinated and slightly unnerved, as Mason surreptitiously glanced around, his gaze lingering on the various passengers, then quickly darting back to the mysterious briefcase. He mumbled something under his breath, a barely audible string of consonants that sounded more like a distressed bird than a coherent sentence. He clutched the briefcase tighter, his knuckles white against the worn leather.

The train lurched violently, throwing Jacob against the seat. A collective gasp went up from the other passengers; a wave of panicked whispers rippled through the car. Jacob grabbed the pole for support, his heart pounding in his chest. Then, the world exploded in a blinding flash of light.

The blinding white light was not a sudden burst but a gradual, all-encompassing increase in intensity, like the sun rising on a scale that defied comprehension. It wasn't painful, just overwhelmingly bright, and it seemed to expand exponentially, filling his senses until he couldn't tell where the light ended and he began. He

instinctively squeezed his eyes shut, instinctively bracing himself for a painful impact. Instead, there was a nauseating feeling of displacement; a sensation of being untethered, of falling, not through space, but through...time. It wasn't a simple transition; it was a chaotic, disorienting process. It felt like the whole world was turning inside out, colors swirling into a vortex of impossible hues, sounds dissolving into a high-pitched, ear-splitting whine. The smell of the subway – the sweat, the metal, the chemicals – all vanished, replaced by a dizzying mix of smells he couldn't quite place.

When he finally opened his eyes, the world had utterly transformed. Gone was the metallic gleam of the subway car, the relentless drone of the tracks, the jostling bodies of fellow passengers. In its place was a world that seemed to belong to another era: a world of cobblestone streets, horse-drawn carriages, and men in threadbare suits. The air, thick with the scent of coal smoke and something akin to desperation, hung heavy in his lungs.

The blinding light was gone, replaced by a dim, dusky twilight that seemed almost unnatural. The sounds were equally different: instead of the mechanical roar of the train, the only sounds to greet

his ears were the clip-clop of horses' hooves on the cobblestones, the rumble of distant carts, and the murmuring voices of people who seemed to be living on the edge of something.

He was standing on a grimy, cobblestone street, surrounded by buildings that looked aged and worn; many were showing obvious signs of decay. Buildings that were not only old but also lacked the gleam of modern architecture. The faint glow of gas lamps flickered in the gathering gloom, casting long, dancing shadows that seemed to writhe with an eerie life of their own. The scene lacked the bright, electric energy of modern New York; there was a tangible sense of poverty and hardship that hung heavy in the air like a suffocating blanket.

Mason Anderson stood beside him, looking equally disoriented and just a tad more terrified. His clothes were still rumpled, but his face, no longer hidden behind nervous fidgeting, was pale and etched with a look of stark apprehension. He pushed his glasses back up his nose, adjusting them with trembling hands.

"Well, that was... unexpected," Mason said, his voice raspy, almost a whisper. "Looks like we took a bit of a detour."

Jacob felt a wave of dizziness wash over him. His mind raced, trying to make sense of what had just happened. The blinding light, the nauseating sensation of falling through time, the sudden, drastic shift in the surrounding environment: it was all too overwhelming, too unbelievable to comprehend. He stared at Mason, trying to decipher whether he was hallucinating. His mind struggled with the impossibility of it all.

"Detour?" Jacob managed, his voice sounding strangely thin and distant even to his own ears. "We're... we're not on the subway anymore." He swallowed hard, the lump in his throat growing with each passing moment.

Mason nodded grimly, his eyes darting around, scanning their surroundings with a mixture of caution and desperation. He opened the mysterious briefcase, revealing a complex array of dials, wires, and glowing tubes. The contraption hummed softly with an almost

sinister energy, each whirring gear and sparking wire seeming to underscore their incredibly precarious situation.

"Time travel isn't exactly comfortable, is it?" Mason stated with a touch of dark humor that was completely out of step with their situation, "And unfortunately, this particular model isn't exactly known for its smooth landings."

"Time... travel?" Jacob echoed, staring at the device with a mixture of disbelief and dawning horror. He looked around, focusing on the details that only now began to register. The clothes, the buildings, the horse-drawn carriages: they all pointed to one inevitable

conclusion. They weren't just on a different street; they were in a different time. The implications of that statement crashed over him with the full force of a tidal wave.

Mason leaned in, his voice dropping to a conspiratorial whisper.

"Let's just say I'm on the run from NASA. They're not too happy about me... borrowing... this little beauty." He patted the briefcase with a somewhat guilty expression.

"NASA?" Jacob sputtered, completely lost in the sudden shift in the narrative. Everything he knew, everything he thought he understood about reality, had been irrevocably shattered in the span of a few terrifying minutes. This was beyond unbelievable. It was absurd. It was...an adventure.

The realization sparked a strange sense of exhilaration, a potent mix of terror and excitement coursing through his veins. He wasn't just attending a funeral; he was stranded in 1929 New York City, on the run from NASA, with a man carrying a time-traveling device. He was living a plot out of one of his favorite science fiction novels.

A Different World

The air, thick with the acrid bite of coal smoke and the cloying sweetness of unwashed bodies, hung heavy in Jacob's lungs. It was a far cry from the sterile, metallic tang of the subway. He coughed, the sound swallowed by the cacophony of the street: the rhythmic clip-clop of horses' hooves on the cobblestones, the rumble of heavy wagons, the cacophony of hawkers vying for attention, their voices a raspy chorus in the gloom. Overhead, a single, sputtering gas lamp cast a sickly yellow glow, painting the grimy cobblestones in an ethereal, unsettling light.

The buildings themselves were a testament to time's relentless march. They were grander, in some respects, than their modern counterparts, boasting ornate detailing and a sense of imposing scale. But the grandeur was tarnished, the stonework crumbling in places, brick mortar flaking, the once-proud facades stained and streaked with grime. Windows were dark and shuttered, hinting at empty interiors and the stark realities of the Great Depression. The overall impression was one of faded glory, a poignant reminder of a past that was both opulent and undeniably broken.

Men in threadbare suits, their faces etched with lines of hardship, hurried past, their shoulders slumped with the weight of their burdens. Women, many with children clinging to their skirts, shuffled along, their eyes downcast, searching for scraps of sustenance. A palpable sense of desperation hung in the air, a silent scream against the backdrop of economic ruin. It was a world far removed from Jacob's comfortable, technology-saturated present. A world that felt both alien and intensely real.

Jacob felt a tremor run through him, not the nervous energy of Mason, but a deeper, visceral reaction to the sheer weight of history surrounding him. He glanced at Mason, who was frantically checking the contents of his briefcase, his brow furrowed in concentration. The device, a chaotic jumble of gleaming metal, wires, and glowing tubes, hummed softly, a counterpoint to the gritty symphony of the street.

"So," Mason said, snapping the briefcase shut with a decisive click, "That was... enlightening. I wasn't expecting this particular century." He offered a wry smile, the humor forced but undeniably present. "Though I suppose the 1920s do have a certain... vintage charm. If you're into that sort of thing."

Jacob managed a weak chuckle, the sound swallowed by the city's roar. "Vintage charm? Mason, we're in 1929. The Great Depression.

This isn't a museum exhibit; it's...real life, with no cell phone signal." He ran a hand through his hair, the gesture as much for comfort as for emphasis. The reality of their situation was starting to sink in, replacing the initial shock with a growing sense of unease.

Mason sighed, running a hand through his already disheveled hair.

"Yes, yes. I'm aware. And let's not even talk about the lack of decent coffee. I need a jolt. A really strong jolt. I need to get this thing calibrated. This jump was...rough." He tapped the briefcase gently. "It's usually far more precise. I blame the subway's electromagnetic field. The damn thing's a temperamental beast, even by time travel standards. It's quite sensitive to unexpected disturbances."

Jacob's eyebrows shot up. "Electromagnetic fields? You think the subway caused this?"

Mason shrugged. "It's a plausible theory, given the circumstances. Believe me, there's more I'd like to explain, but we need a safer place for a more thorough debriefing. What time is it?" He produced a rather battered pocket watch from his vest. Jacob noticed several smaller pouches and compartments subtly hidden in the clothing. It looked like he'd been expecting a rough journey.

"I don't know. My watch...I think I left it on the subway," Jacob said, feeling a wave of ridiculousness wash over him. He'd lost track of time, quite literally. The time-traveling itself had been disorienting; the jarring transition had left him with a lingering sense of vertigo.

"Don't worry about your watch," Mason said, checking the time. "It's a bit late in the afternoon, but I think I know a place where we can sort of hide out and get a better idea of what to do. It's not the Waldorf-Astoria, but it's got character." He gave a strained smile. "It's been a while since I've been out in the field. There's a whole lot of things I'd love to tell you, but not out here."

As Mason led Jacob through the labyrinthine streets, the grim reality of 1929 New York pressed in on them. The sights, sounds, and smells were relentless, a visceral assault on their senses. The air, thick with coal smoke and the stench of poverty, was a stark contrast to the relative cleanliness of their own time. They passed by breadlines, where gaunt men and women waited patiently for meager rations. Ragged children, their eyes hollow with hunger, scavenged for scraps in the gutters. The contrast between this poverty-stricken landscape and the abundance of Jacob's life was striking.

The place Mason took him to wasn't grand, but rather a small, unassuming apartment building. The building's entrance showed signs of neglect, the paint peeling and chipping, the steps worn and uneven. The stairs creaked ominously under their weight. Mason produced a key from another hidden pouch, fumbling with the lock before the door opened with a rusty groan. The air inside was stuffy and stale, but at least it was relatively safe and quiet.

Once inside, Mason finally had a chance to offer some semblance of explanation. He spoke of a clandestine NASA program, a project that had gone horribly wrong, a device that was more powerful than anyone had anticipated. He spoke of colleagues who were driven by ambition and ruthlessness and of the potential dangers involved with the time travel technology. He spoke of the ethical implications, of the potential paradoxes, of the immense responsibility that rested on his shoulders. He explained how he'd recovered the device from the wreckage of the space shuttle "Prospector", not for personal gain but to prevent it from falling into the wrong hands, to save it from misuse.

"The device," Mason continued, "it's more than just a machine; it's...a paradox wrapped in a paradox. It's powerful, unpredictable, and frankly, dangerous. One wrong move, a slight miscalculation, and you could unravel the very fabric of reality. I'm running from NASA, not because I've done something wrong. I believe they intend to weaponize this technology. And I won't let that happen. Not on my watch."

Jacob listened, absorbing the torrent of information, his mind struggling to reconcile the fantastical narrative with the gritty reality of their surroundings. The Great Depression served as a stark backdrop to their science fiction adventure. He was far from the comfortable familiarity of his own life, thrown into a chaotic maelstrom of time travel, political intrigue, and the harsh realities of the 1930s. The sheer improbability of it all, the sheer weight of it all, left him breathless. This was not just a trip to his great-uncle's funeral; it was an adventure beyond his wildest dreams. Or perhaps, his worst nightmares.

Meeting the uncles

The alley reeked of stale beer, rotting garbage, and something vaguely animalistic. Mason, ever the pragmatist, consulted his battered pocket watch again. "Right then," he muttered, "Let's find these... relatives of yours." He consulted a crumpled piece of paper, his brow furrowed in concentration. "According to the somewhat sketchy information I gleaned from your... uh... rather unconventional method of obtaining family history," he gestured vaguely towards Jacob, "we're looking for a pair of struggling artists, living somewhere near... this." He pointed to a barely legible address scribbled on the paper.

The address led them to a dilapidated tenement building, its paint peeling like sunburnt skin, the windows grimy and opaque. A single bare bulb cast a weak, flickering light over the entrance, illuminating cracked plaster and crumbling stone. The air hung heavy with the smell of dampness, despair, and something akin to despairing hope clinging stubbornly to its edges.

Climbing the rickety stairs, each step groaning a protest under their weight, Jacob felt a knot tighten in his stomach. He wasn't sure what he expected to find, but it certainly wasn't this. The building seemed to breathe with the collective sighs of its inhabitants, each creak and groan a testament to poverty and neglect. He glanced at Mason, whose expression was one of grim determination.

They reached the third floor, the air growing thicker with the smell of paint thinner and turpentine. Mason knocked on a door, the sound muffled by the layers of dust and decay. A moment of tense silence followed, broken only by the distant rumble of city traffic and the rhythmic drip, drip, drip of a leaky faucet somewhere within the building.

The door opened slowly, revealing a gaunt man with kind eyes and a shock of unruly gray hair. He wore a paint-splattered shirt, his hands stained with the residue of his craft, his gaze weary yet

sharp. Beside him, a younger man, his face etched with similar lines of worry, peered out from behind him, his own hands clutching a paintbrush.

"Can I help you?" the older man asked, his voice raspy, like sandpaper against wood.

Mason cleared his throat, "Actually, yes. I believe you are... Uncle Elias and Uncle Arthur Walker?" The question hung in the air, heavy with the weight of both hope and the absurd reality of their situation.

The older man, Elias, looked at them both carefully, sizing them up before he answered cautiously. "That's us, although we wouldn't know you from Adam. Are you with the landlord? If so, I'm sorry, we're a little late with rent."

Jacob felt a surge of empathy for these men, strangers to him yet undeniably his relatives. "No, sir, no, we're not from the landlord," Jacob said, feeling awkward. "My name is Jacob Walker. I'm... I'm a relative. A great-nephew, actually." He felt a blush creep onto his cheeks, the statement absurd and improbable. It was as if he'd stepped into a scene from a play, a poorly written play at that.

Elias and Arthur exchanged a look, a mixture of skepticism and bewilderment crossing their faces. Arthur, the younger of the two, spoke up. "A great-nephew? We haven't heard from anyone in... well, a long time."

The silence stretched between them, heavy with unspoken questions and implied history. Jacob, unsure of how to proceed, pulled out the two hundred dollars his mom had given him earlier. "I... I wanted to give this to you," he stammered, offering the money. "I know things are difficult..."

He also pulled out the silver dollar, the one he found at the entrance to the subway. It had become a symbol of this bizarre adventure – a tangible link to the improbable chain of events. He presented it to Elias with a trembling hand. "And... this," he added, as an afterthought.

The look of bewilderment on their faces shifted, replaced by a strange mixture of wonder and cautious hope. Elias gently took both the money and the coin, his fingers tracing the worn surface

of the silver dollar. He examined it closely, his eyes widening as he did so.

"Where... where did you get this?" Elias whispered, his voice barely audible. He looked at the coin again as if trying to remember something he had long forgotten. "This...this is..." he trailed off, seemingly lost in his thoughts.

Arthur, equally perplexed, stared at Jacob and Mason in turn, his gaze darting between the two young men. He asked, "Who are you, exactly? And how did you get this coin?"

Jacob realized that he'd stumbled into a situation far deeper and more complex than he had imagined. The silver dollar - a seemingly insignificant detail in the grand scheme of their time travel

escapade – seemed to hold a significance he didn't yet understand. This was more than just a chance encounter; it was a convergence of past and present, of family and fate, entwined in a web of historical mystery.

The two uncles led them into their cramped apartment, a space barely larger than a walk-in closet. The walls were lined with canvases, some finished, others half-painted, reflecting a life dedicated to art, even in the midst of grinding poverty. The air was thick with the scent of turpentine and linseed oil, a familiar comfort in the heart of their desperate struggle. They offered Jacob and Mason chipped mugs of lukewarm coffee, a gesture of hospitality in the face of their own hardships.

They talked about their struggles. Elias spoke of his dreams, of commissions lost to the economic downturn, of the sacrifices he had made to keep his art alive. Arthur echoed his brother's sentiments, sharing the same hardships, though he was less inclined to dwell on what he considered foolish dreams. They spoke of the hardships of the era, of the hunger, the evictions, the constant fear of losing everything. They spoke of their shared grief over their brother's loss, a loss that seemed to have broken their spirits even further.

Jacob listened, his heart aching for their plight. He felt a kinship with them, a connection that transcended the vast gulf of time

and

the unusual circumstances of their meeting.

The conversation meandered, drifting from the immediate hardships of their present to the shared memories of their brother, Jacob's great-uncle. The stories painted a vivid portrait of a man who, despite the challenges he faced, possessed a sharp intellect and a remarkable ability to spot opportunity. They talked of his

investments, his dreams, his quiet optimism even in the face of adversity. Their memories of him were shrouded in a haze of

poverty but imbued with a strong sense of his optimism, which felt oddly at odds with their current circumstances. The tales sparked a curiosity within Jacob, a feeling of almost nostalgic sadness for a man he never knew, yet suddenly felt profoundly connected to.

As the evening drew to a close, the uncles expressed gratitude for Jacob's unexpected generosity. The two hundred dollars wouldn't solve their problems, but it would certainly provide some respite. The significance of the silver dollar, however, remained unspoken yet palpable. It hung in the air between them, a silent question waiting for an answer, a key to a mystery that seemed to have its roots planted deep in the past. Jacob, leaving their cramped apartment, felt a profound sense of connection to these men, to this time, to this unexpectedly entwined family history. He left with a heavier heart, a deeper understanding of the past, and the persistent nagging feeling that the silver dollar held the key to much more than just a family secret. The adventure, it seemed, was only just beginning.

Escape from the Past

The air in the cramped apartment hung thick with the unspoken weight of the silver dollar. Elias, his gaze distant and preoccupied, traced the worn surface of the coin with a trembling finger. Arthur, ever the pragmatist, was less enthralled by the antique, his concern centered on their immediate financial predicament. "So, this...great-nephew thing," he began, his voice a low rumble, "how does that work?"

Jacob, still reeling from the unexpected turn of events, tried to explain the impossible. He recounted the bizarre chain of events, the accidental activation of the time-traveling device, the whirlwind journey through time, the frantic search for his relatives, all leading to this improbable encounter. He spoke of Mason, his reluctant companion, and the device itself, a cobbled-together contraption of gleaming brass, sparking wires, and whirring gears. He felt the need to convince them, to justify his presence, his story. Yet, he knew that no amount of explanation could fully capture the seriality of his experience.

As he spoke, the room felt as though it shrank around them. The shadows, elongated by the weak light of the single bare bulb, seemed to press in. The previously comforting smell of turpentine and linseed oil had been replaced by a heavy, oppressive silence, broken only by the rhythmic ticking of a grandfather clock in the corner, a stark counterpoint to the breathless urgency of Jacob's narrative.

He finished, his voice trailing off, his gaze falling to the worn wooden floorboards. He'd laid bare his fantastical journey, a tale that should've been met with skepticism, with outright disbelief. Yet, the uncles' expressions were unreadable, their gazes locked on the silver dollar.

Finally, Elias spoke, his voice a low whisper. "This coin... it belonged to my brother, Silas. He disappeared... vanished without a trace... almost two years ago." He looked at Jacob, a glimmer of recognition flickering in his eyes. "He often spoke of... of investments, of opportunities... of a future he felt was just around the corner."

Arthur nodded; a somber expression etched on his face. "Silas always had a head for business, a knack for spotting a good deal. He believed in the impossible, you know. Always dreaming big." He paused, his gaze falling to the floor. "But after he disappeared, the world stopped dreaming for us. We... we just tried to survive."

The weight of their shared history settled upon the room like a shroud. Jacob felt a profound sense of understanding, a realization that his own wild adventure was intertwined with a mystery that spanned generations. The silver dollar wasn't just a key; it was a link, a tangible connection across the chasm of time.

The conversation shifted. They spoke of Silas's life, his ambitions, his unfinished dreams. From their recollections, a portrait emerged– a man of brilliant intellect, restless spirit, and unyielding

optimism. A man who saw potential in a world that seemed to offer only despair. His investments, once a source of hope, had become a mystery, a puzzle with missing pieces. The silver dollar, a memento from a deal that had gone awry, was the only clue they had left.

Mason, who had remained a silent observer, cleared his throat. "So, this... coin," he said, his voice practical, "does it lead to this... investment?"

Elias, seeming to emerge from a reverie, nodded. "It's all I have left. Silas always said it would lead him to fortune. He never explained it, only that it was a key...a keystone to something..." at that moment Elias hands the coin back to Jacob and said, "here take this, it appears you are family, and it will serve as a memory of our meeting here today!"

Mason, with a gleam in his eye, examined the coin closely. "It's... peculiar. The inscription... I think I can see a faint mark here. It looks like...coordinates?"

While Mason meticulously examined the coin, revealing a series of almost imperceptible markings under the dim light, Jacob found himself swept away in a tide of conflicting emotions. Relief at connecting with his family, a sense of responsibility towards the predicament they found themselves in, and a palpable sense of foreboding as the ramifications of their actions began to truly sink in. He thought back to the initial chaos of their arrival, the hurried escape, the pursuit by the seemingly omniscient authorities. Now, they had a new, urgent mission. Find Silas's lost investment, understand the significance of the silver dollar, and perhaps, just perhaps, repair the rip in time they'd inadvertently created.

Jacob thanked the men for the gift, their hospitiality and bidded them farewell, and left his great uncles, in the mysterious time frame.

The time to celebrate was over. Mason, his usual reticence replaced by a grim focus, began to reassemble his device. The clatter of metal against metal, the whirring of gears, and the occasional spark from a frayed wire filled the small apartment with the sounds of their desperate race against time. The air grew thick with

anticipation, a mixture of excitement and trepidation.

He worked with intense concentration, his fingers flying over the complex mechanisms. He muttered to himself, his words a blend of technical jargon and frustrated sighs. The work was meticulous, requiring immense precision. One wrong move could render the device useless, or worse, catastrophic.

"Alright," he finally announced, wiping a smudge of grease from his forehead. "She's ready, but we need to move fast. The chronometer shows a temporal anomaly rapidly forming. Staying here is too risky."

He gestured towards a small, almost hidden panel on the side of the machine. "There's a short window to make our jump. Any interference from the temporal police, or any deviation from the precise coordinates, could be... unpleasant." His voice carried a heavy undertone of foreboding.

The alleyway outside was even more sinister under the cloak of the city's nighttime cover. The air hung thick with shadows and the smell of damp concrete, the sounds of the city only amplifying the quiet urgency of their escape. The risks were substantial. Getting caught meant imprisonment, or worse, oblivion.

As Mason initiated the jump sequence, the device hummed, vibrated, and thrummed with a power that seemed almost alive. Lights flashed, gears whirred at an alarming speed, and wires sparked brilliantly, casting flickering shadows against the grimy walls of the alleyway. Jacob gripped the device's stabilizing bar, feeling the surge of energy coursing through it, a tangible echo of the temporal displacement they were about to undertake.

Suddenly, a harsh spotlight cut through the darkness, accompanied by the sharp barks of what sounded like trained police dogs. Mason reacted instantly, plunging the device into a mode he referred to as "stealth" and cursing under his breath. The alleyway was now the scene of a frantic chase. They darted between overflowing garbage bins and dilapidated buildings, the sounds of pursuing footsteps echoing behind them, blending with the increasingly intense hum of the time-traveling machine.

The alley's maze-like structure provided some cover, but the pursuing officers seemed to have the alley's layout memorized. Mason muttered about the temporal anomalies he'd previously observed, suspecting they might have alerted the authorities to their presence.

Their race against time was intensified, each heartbeat a frantic drumbeat. The machine's chronometer was rapidly counting down, indicating a rapidly diminishing opportunity for a safe jump. The device sputtered, then lurched forward, as if struggling against the forces of time itself. Finally, with a violent surge of power, it activated. They were enveloped in a blinding flash of light and deafening roar, and then... nothingness. They'd made the jump, their escape was successful, but the adventure was far from over.

The silver dollar's mystery, the pursuit of Silas Walker's elusive fortune, and the threat of the temporal police all remained unresolved threads in the tapestry of their extraordinary journey. The past, it seemed, was still trying to reclaim them.

Back to the Present

The world slammed back into focus with the jarring intensity of a punch to the gut. One moment, they were hurtling through the swirling vortex of time, the next, they were sprawled in a grimy New York alley, the reek of garbage and damp concrete assaulting their nostrils. The cacophony of the city – the screech of tires, the blare of car horns, the shouts of street vendors – was a stark contrast to the hushed, almost reverent silence of Silas Walker's dusty attic. Jacob's ears rang, a persistent, high-pitched whine that vibrated deep within his skull.

Mason, ever the pragmatist, was already on his feet, checking the time-traveling device. He muttered something about temporal residue and recalibration, his voice tight with a nervous energy that mirrored Jacob's own. The device, a chaotic jumble of gleaming brass and sparking wires, seemed to hum with a faint, residual energy, a ghostly echo of their journey. He looked like he hadn't slept in days. The grease smudges on his face were now mingled with grime from the alley. His eyes held a weary look.

Jacob, however, remained rooted to the spot, his body trembling with the aftereffects of the temporal jump. The disorientation was overwhelming. The air felt thick, heavy, as if the very fabric of reality itself was still adjusting to their presence. His senses were on overload – the vibrant colors of the city, the cacophony of sounds, the myriads of smells, all assaulting his senses with brutal intensity.

It was as if his perception had been recalibrated, and the present world felt alien, almost hostile, compared to the muted tones and slower pace of the 1920s. He felt an echoing numbness in his extremities.

The world around him seemed to shimmer slightly, as if the edges of reality were still blurring. He blinked, trying to clear his vision, but the slight blurring persisted, a persistent reminder of the dimensional upheaval they had just endured. He felt a throbbing headache coming on.

"Are you alright?" Mason asked, his voice laced with concern. He extended a hand, his touch surprisingly steady despite the chaos of their escape.

Jacob managed a weak nod, the movement causing a fresh wave of dizziness. He took Mason's hand, feeling the reassuring strength in his grip. He wasn't sure how long it took to regain his composure, but when he could stand without stumbling, the first thing he felt was a desperate need to wash the grime of the alley off himself.

"We need to get cleaned up," Jacob croaked, his voice hoarse. The words tasted like ash in his mouth.

Mason nodded, his gaze sweeping the alley. "And we need to get to that will reading," he added, his expression grim. "The sooner we know what Silas left behind, the better. The temporal police won't be far behind, and they won't be happy that we escaped."

The thought sent a fresh wave of anxiety through Jacob. He hadn't even begun to process the emotional and physical fallout from their journey through time, and already the threat of a high-tech police force was looming over them. The escape, while successful, had left them vulnerable, exposed, and deeply exhausted.

They found a dingy all-night diner a few blocks away, the bright fluorescent lights offering a stark contrast to the shadowy alleyway they'd just escaped. The greasy aroma of coffee and stale bacon hung in the air, and the murmur of late-night conversations washed over them. Jacob felt like he was walking through a film reel playing at double speed.

Over lukewarm coffee and suspiciously grey bacon, they discussed their next move. The will reading was scheduled for noon, giving them a few hours to regroup and prepare. Jacob's mind raced, his thoughts a jumbled mess of fragmented memories and pressing anxieties. The contrast between the past and the present was disorienting, the jarring transition a visceral reminder of their extraordinary journey. He hadn't had a chance to fully process his encounter with his great-uncles; their stories, their faces, their shared sorrow, were like a vivid dream.

The city, once a familiar background hum, felt alien. The rush of people, the incessant noise, even the smells – it all felt different, heightened, as if his senses had been sharpened to an unbearable degree by the experience. He felt utterly drained, his mind swimming with the echo of past voices, the scent of old wood, and the chill of the 1920s winter air. It was difficult to reconcile the gritty reality of his present surroundings with the sepia-toned world he'd just left behind. The past still clung to him, a stubborn ghost in the machinery of his present.

He thought about Silas, the man he'd never known, yet somehow felt intimately connected to. The ghost of a smile danced across his lips as he recalled the optimistic gleam in Elias's eye when he spoke of his brother's unwavering belief in the impossible. It was a belief that had echoed through the decades, surviving even the crushing weight of disappointment and loss.

Mason, meanwhile, was meticulously cleaning and recalibrating his device. He worked with the focused intensity of a surgeon, his movements precise and deliberate. He kept glancing at his wristwatch, a silent countdown to the will reading.

As the hands crept closer to noon, a nervous energy settled over Jacob. The anticipation was palpable, a mixture of excitement and trepidation. What would they find in Silas's will? What secrets lay hidden within its pages? And more importantly, would it provide them with the answers they desperately sought, or would it lead them deeper into the labyrinth of mystery and danger?

The taxi ride to the law office felt surreal. The city's relentless energy was a stark contrast to the quiet anticipation in the back seat. He stared out at the buildings, momentarily disoriented, as if he wasn't fully present. The city's noise and sights seemed distant, his focus entirely on the impending confrontation with the unknown. The silver dollar, nestled securely in his pocket, felt cold against his skin – a tangible link to the past, a key to a future still uncertain.

They arrived at the law firm, a imposing building of granite and glass, a monument to wealth and legal expertise. The lobby was pristine, polished to a high sheen, a sharp contrast to the grimy alleyway and the dilapidated diner where they'd sought refuge. The air hummed with an air of quiet efficiency, and Jacob felt a sudden wave of unease. He had a strange feeling that he wasn't entirely ready for what awaited him inside. The echoes of the past lingered, still clinging to him like a persistent shadow. He felt the weight of generations bearing down on him, the collective hopes and

disappointments of a family haunted by a vanished fortune and a cryptic silver dollar. He entered the building, his heart pounding a rhythm of anticipation and fear. The will reading was about to begin, and with it, a new chapter in their extraordinary adventure.

The Silver Dollar

The mahogany table gleamed under the harsh fluorescent lights of the lawyer's office, reflecting the nervous energy that thrummed in the room. Mr. Fitzwilliam, a man whose face seemed permanently etched with the weariness of a thousand legal battles, cleared his throat, the sound echoing in the hushed silence. He adjusted his spectacles, his gaze sweeping over the assembled family members –Mason, stiff and alert beside Jacob, and two elderly men, Elias and Samuel, Jacob's great-uncles, their faces etched with a mixture of anticipation and apprehension.

"The will of Silas Walker," Mr. Fitzwilliam began, his voice a low, measured monotone, "states clearly his desire for his assets to be distributed according to the terms herein outlined." He paused, flipping a page of the legal document, the rustling sound like a whisper in the heavy silence. The lawyer's voice, though calm, carried a subtle undercurrent of formality that underscored the weight of the occasion. His words hung in the air, each syllable carrying the weight of decades of secrets, hopes, and unspoken family history. The atmosphere was thick, heavy, pregnant with the unspoken expectations of those assembled.

He detailed the specifics of Silas's estate – the modest apartment, the modest savings account, the seemingly insignificant personal effects. As he read, a mounting tension filled the room, a tangible entity that made the air crackle. The lawyer droned on about stocks, bonds, and obscure investments, details that seemed to blur into the background as the anticipation mounted. Jacob shifted in his seat, the silver dollar in his pocket a cold, heavy weight against his thigh. He felt a tremor of apprehension, a knot tightening in his stomach.

Then, unexpectedly, the lawyer's voice changed. It lost its monotone, a slight tremor entering his usually controlled speech. He seemed to stumble over a phrase, his words hesitant, almost stumbling. "And lastly," he said, his voice barely a whisper, "a... a curious item is mentioned. A silver dollar, specifically, bearing the date 1929, described as..." he paused, glancing down at the will again, his eyes widening slightly, "...described as 'a token of profound significance.'"

A sudden silence descended upon the room, heavier now than before. The lawyer looked up, his eyes meeting Jacob's. A flicker of surprise, of something akin to disbelief, crossed his features.

Elias and Samuel, Jacob's great-uncles, exchanged a look. It was a look of stunned recognition, of sudden understanding, a silent conversation passing between them that Jacob couldn't quite decipher. Then, with a movement that seemed almost involuntary, Elias reached into his waistcoat pocket, slowly pulling out a worn, leather pouch. He opened it, revealing a single, tarnished silver dollar – a 1929 Peace dollar. He held it up, the light catching its dulled surface, bringing out the subtle details of the design.

Samuel mirrored the action, producing an identical coin from his own pocket. The two coins, almost mirror images of each other, lay side by side, reflecting the shared history of their family. The silence in the room amplified, the only sound the soft rustling of the old leather pouches.

Jacob felt a jolt, a sudden, inexplicable surge of adrenaline. He could feel his heart pounding in his ears, a rapid, frantic beat that resonated through his entire body. He glanced down at his own pocket, his fingers instinctively touching the silver dollar nestled there. He could feel the cool, smooth surface of the metal against his skin, a strange sensation of connection between himself, the two coins, and his great-uncles. It felt profoundly significant, even more profound than it had when he first found it in Silas's attic.

Suddenly Jacob reaches in his pocket, lifts the coin out and tosses it on the table.

Mr. Fitzwilliam, seeming completely baffled by this sudden turn of events, stammered, "I... I didn't... I wasn't aware of this..."

Elias and Samuel were lost in a hushed conversation, their voices low and urgent, but their words completely unintelligible to Jacob and Mason. The two elderly men exchanged increasingly agitated glances. Their initial astonishment seemed to transform into an excited bewilderment, and finally into a near-manic intensity. Jacob noticed that one of them was subtly wiping the dust and tarnish off

the coin.

Mason leaned towards Jacob, his voice barely a whisper. "Did you... give them those coins?" he asked, his eyes wide with disbelief. His tone carried a strange mixture of incredulity and a certain fascination, his voice laced with an almost palpable curiosity. He shifted in his seat, his eyes darting between the coins, the uncles, and Jacob. His usually pragmatic demeanor seemed to falter slightly as the gravity of the situation sunk in.

Jacob, his mind racing to catch up with the sudden, unexpected revelation. The memory flooded back – a cold December day in 1929, a chance encounter in a bustling

marketplace, a fleeting moment of kindness to two elderly strangers. He remembered the way their eyes had lit up, a spark of hope in their tired gaze, when he had presented them with the tarnished silver dollar, a gesture that at the time seemed almost insignificant.

"I... I gave them two hundred dollars, and the coin, but they gave it back to me," Jacob confirmed, his voice barely a breath. "It was a long time ago, in New York... a Christmas Eve. "The memory felt extraordinarily vivid, the details – the smell of roasting chestnuts, the snow falling softly, the joyful chatter of the crowd – painting a picture in his mind that was incredibly sharp and detailed. The memory came flooding back, surprising him in its accuracy and intensity. He'd completely forgotten the event.

The revelation hung in the air, a charged silence that was suddenly broken by Elias's sharp intake of breath. He looked at Jacob, his eyes shining with something akin to awe. "Silas," he breathed, his voice trembling slightly. "Silas always said..." He paused, his eyes filling with tears. "After you came to visit us, Silas came back home, he was leaving and going back out west. We told him about your visit, and he took one hundred dollars, of the two hundred you left us, and took it with him as he left.He always said the impossible is possible. He never explained. He merely said, keep the faith, it'll all make sense.

He just never said when. Our father before he died, left each of his sons a 1929 silver dollar. That's why all of us had one!"

Samuel nodded vigorously, his own eyes glistening with unshed tears. He looked at Jacob, his expression a mixture of wonder and relief. "He never told us what he found out on his journey through the world. That he'd found the meaning to this very coin. This very day. You, you changed everything." He choked back a sob. "We thought it was a simple act of kindness, from one stranger to another. We always wondered why we found ourselves thinking so strongly about him over the years. We just thought our old age made it more poignant."

The weight of their words crashed down on Jacob, the significance of his seemingly insignificant act of kindness suddenly taking on enormous proportions. It wasn't merely a forgotten act of charity, but a pivotal event that had set in motion a chain of events that transcended time and circumstance. The silver dollar, once a simple piece of change, had become a key, unlocking not only a family legacy but a gateway to a world Jacob had never imagined. The seemingly random encounter in a bustling Christmas Eve marketplace decades ago had woven itself into the fabric of Silas Walker's final will and testament, a testament to the power of unexpected connections and the enduring strength of hope.

The lawyer, still visibly shaken, cleared his throat again, his voice regaining some of its earlier composure, though a tremor still remained. "I... I believe," he said slowly, "I believe we need to... reconsider this will. The implications... are far more significant than I initially anticipated."

The air crackled with unspoken possibilities, a swirling vortex of questions and anticipations. What would the full implications of Silas's last words and the silver dollar mean? What mysteries lay hidden behind this sudden, unexpected revelation? The answers remained shrouded in uncertainty, but one thing was clear: Jacob's life, already altered by his journey through time, was about to change irrevocably, propelled by a single, tarnished silver dollar and a moment of kindness that had echoed across the decades. The weight of Silas's legacy, and the secrets it held, were finally beginning to unveil themselves, the consequences unpredictable and potentially profound.

Unexpected Inheritance

Mr. Fitzwilliam, still visibly flustered, adjusted his glasses, a nervous tic he'd displayed throughout the reading of the will. He cleared his throat, the sound surprisingly loud in the sudden silence that had fallen over the room. The air, thick with anticipation a moment before, now felt charged with something entirely different– a potent cocktail of shock, disbelief, and a burgeoning sense of awe. He tapped a pen against the leather-bound will, the rhythmic tapping a stark counterpoint to the racing thoughts in Jacob's head.

"However," Mr. Fitzwilliam began, his voice a little shaky, "there is a... a further clause. A rather... unusual one." He paused, his gaze sweeping across the faces assembled around the mahogany table. His eyes lingered on Jacob, whose mind was still reeling from the unexpected significance of the silver dollar. The lawyer's hesitation only served to amplify the already palpable tension in the room.

He cleared his throat again, then launched into a recitation of details that were initially incomprehensible to Jacob, a series of corporate names, stock symbols, and figures that danced in his peripheral vision like a confusing financial ballet. Jacob strained to listen, each word a puzzle piece that stubbornly refused to fit into any coherent picture. He felt his heart quicken again, the adrenaline still coursing through his veins. Was this another layer to the

mystery of the silver dollar? Another unexpected twist?

Then, like a bolt of lightning, clarity struck. Mr. Fitzwilliam's voice, though still measured, had gained a new resonance, a certain gravitas that pierced through the initial confusion. He spoke of extensive oil holdings, of wells in Texas, of pipelines stretching across continents, of a vast network of holdings that spanned

decades and continents. He talked of billions, not millions, a wealth that Jacob had never even dreamed possible.

The numbers, previously meaningless, snapped into sharp focus. The pieces of the puzzle clicked together with a satisfying *thunk* , revealing a picture that left Jacob breathless. His great-uncles, Elias and Samuel, were not merely living on modest pensions, they were

sitting atop a fortune—a fortune of astronomical proportions. And according to the will, the entirety of this vast fortune, this unexpected and unimaginable wealth, was bequeathed to him – Jacob.

A collective gasp filled the room. Mason, beside Jacob, stared at him, his mouth open in silent astonishment. His face, usually so stoic and reserved, was a mask of sheer disbelief. Elias and Samuel, after their initial stunned silence, exchanged a look that contained a mixture of surprise and something akin to profound, almost

mystical relief. Then Elias, his hand trembling slightly, reached out and laid a hand on Jacob's shoulder.

"Silas," Elias said, his voice thick with emotion, "he... he always knew."

Samuel nodded, his eyes shimmering with tears, his face a study of quiet joy. "He knew. He always believed in you, Jacob. He never doubted for a moment that you were the one."

Jacob, overwhelmed, could only stare at them, his mind struggling to process the torrent of information that was flooding his senses. He felt numb, a strange combination of shock and incredulity washing over him. One moment, he was a struggling artist, burdened with debt and uncertainty; the next, he was the sole heir to a vast fortune, a fortune that dwarfed his wildest imagination. The enormity of it all was slowly, gradually dawning on him. He was rich. Immensely rich. A sudden, unexpected billionaire. The very idea was so alien, so fantastical, that it felt surreal. It was like stepping into a dream, a dream so vivid and intensely real that he couldn't distinguish between fantasy and reality. He ran a hand through his hair, feeling the shock ripples through him.

Mr. Fitzwilliam, sensing the profound impact of his revelation, cleared his throat once more, his voice regaining some of its professional composure. He explained the mechanics of the inheritance, the legal procedures, the tax implications – details that seemed almost insignificant in the face of the overwhelming reality. Jacob barely registered the words, his mind still grappling with the

sheer scale of his unexpected fortune.

Mason, after a period of stunned silence, broke the spell, his voice surprisingly calm considering the circumstances. "So... you're a billionaire, then?" he asked, a hint of awe in his voice, a stark contrast to his usual pragmatism. There was a certain amount of respectful jealousy in his voice. "That's... quite something." He sounded genuinely pleased for Jacob, despite the sheer scale of it all.

Elias and Samuel, having composed themselves somewhat, smiled at Jacob, their faces alight with a joy that seemed to radiate warmth through the entire room. They had found their missing piece. The meaning of their long wait, the mystery of the coin. It had all centered around Jacob, the young man who had unwittingly set into motion a cascade of events that reached across decades.

They had waited patiently. They had kept the faith, as Silas had always encouraged.

"It's... it's hard to believe," Jacob finally managed to say, his voice trembling slightly. The words felt inadequate, a feeble attempt to articulate the storm of emotions raging within him. He glanced down at the silver dollar in his pocket, a simple coin that had become the linchpin of this extraordinary chain of events. It felt almost sacred now. The weight of it was immense, both literally and metaphorically.

Mr. Fitzwilliam continued to explain the details of the will, but Jacob's attention drifted. He was lost in a whirlwind of thoughts, struggling to make sense of this incredible turn of events. His life, already irrevocably altered by his journey through time, had just undergone another seismic shift. His future, once shrouded in uncertainty, was now painted in strokes of unimaginable wealth and possibilities.

The weight of the oil fortune, the implications of this unexpected inheritance, were slowly sinking in. He wondered about the responsibility that came with such wealth, the potential impact on his life, and the lives of those around him. He thought about his art, his dreams, his future plans. Would this change everything?

As the lawyer concluded his explanation, Jacob felt a mixture of excitement, apprehension, and a profound sense of bewilderment. The room around him seemed to swim, the faces of his great-uncles, Mason, and even Mr. Fitzwilliam, blurring slightly at the edges. The silver dollar, nestled against his thigh, felt heavy, a tangible link to the past, the present, and the uncertain future that lay before him. He had stumbled into an extraordinary adventure, a journey fueled by a single, tarnished silver dollar and the money he left his uncles, and the unexpected legacy of his great-uncle Silas Walker. Silas had taken the one hundred dollars, and invested it. He had unwittingly changed their lives, and this extraordinary inheritance would inevitably change his own. The adventure had only just begun.

Family Reactions

The news hung in the air, thick and suffocating, a miasma of disbelief and stunned silence. Then, the dam broke. Chaos, beautiful and terrifying, erupted.

Aunt Mildred, who hadn't spoken a word throughout the entire will reading, let out a shriek that could curdle milk. She clutched at her pearls, her face a mask of horrified delight. "Billions?" she squawked, her voice cracking with a strange mixture of hysteria and elation. "Jacob, you... you're a billionaire! Oh, my stars!" She fainted dramatically, collapsing into the arms of a bewildered Uncle Edgar, who muttered something about needing smelling salts and a stiff drink.

Uncle Edgar, ever the pragmatist, had a different kind of shock. His initial reaction wasn't one of awe, but of suspicion. He adjusted his spectacles, his eyes narrowed in a way that suggested he was already formulating a complex legal strategy. "Are you certain, Fitzwilliam?" he questioned, his voice sharp and precise. "Absolutely certain about the... the provenance of these assets? There might be... complications." He looked suspiciously at Elias and Samuel, a glint of calculating skepticism in his eyes. He smelled a rat, or perhaps a very large, very lucrative, oil well.

Cousin Penelope, ever the drama queen, burst into tears – tears of both joy and envy, it was hard to tell which. She wailed, "Oh, Jacob, darling! This is simply marvelous! Though, I must admit, I always suspected there was something...special about you." Her eyes darted towards Mason, a calculating glint replacing the theatrical tears. Mason, ever stoic, merely raised an eyebrow. Penelope's strategic weeping was, frankly, nothing new.

Mason, despite his initial awe, quickly regained his composure. He was a practical man, a man of numbers and spreadsheets. He moved closer to Jacob, a quiet smile playing on his lips. "Well, Jacob," he said, clapping Jacob on the shoulder with surprising force,

"Congratulations. Let's discuss investment strategies. I've got a few ideas..." His eyes shone with a controlled excitement, the glint of a

seasoned financial strategist recognizing a once-in-a-lifetime opportunity. He was already mentally calculating percentages, returns, and long-term growth plans. His quiet celebration was far more intimidating than Penelope's histrionics.

Meanwhile, Elias and Samuel, having weathered the initial storm of disbelief, were basking in a quiet joy. They watched the unfolding family drama with a detached amusement, their eyes twinkling with a knowing smile. Their relief was palpable. The weight of a

decades-long secret, the silent burden of Silas Walker's cryptic clues, was finally lifted. They had kept the faith, nurtured the hope, and now, against all odds, their trust in their nephew had been

vindicated. Their long and patient waiting had paid off in ways they had only dreamed of. Elias took Jacob's hand, his own calloused fingers surprisingly gentle. He didn't need words; the unspoken understanding between them spoke volumes.

Jacob, however, was completely overwhelmed. The sheer scale of the fortune, the sudden shift in his life, was almost too much to bear. He felt like he was standing on the edge of a precipice, staring into an abyss of unimaginable wealth and responsibility. The silver dollar in his pocket felt heavier than ever, a tangible reminder of the extraordinary chain of events that had led him to this moment.

His mother, usually a whirlwind of energy, was strangely subdued.

She stared at him, her eyes wide and unblinking, as if trying to process something beyond her comprehension. A silent tear traced a path down her weathered cheek. She had always believed in Jacob, always supported his artistic aspirations, even when others doubted him. This sudden windfall, this astonishing turn of events, left her speechless, overwhelmed by a mixture of pride, relief, and a nagging fear of how this might change her son.

His father, a gruff and taciturn man of few words, surprised everyone by embracing Jacob in a bear hug that nearly cracked his ribs. He patted Jacob's back, his usually stoic demeanor broken by a rare display of emotion. A single tear escaped his eye, quickly brushed away with the back of his hand. He mumbled something about being proud, a sentiment that meant the world to Jacob. The unspoken bond of father and son, forged through years of shared struggle, was strengthened by this incredible turn of fortune.

Even Mr. Fitzwilliam, the normally unflappable lawyer, seemed a bit shaken. He looked around the room, a faint smile playing on his lips as he witnessed the chaos he had inadvertently unleashed. He knew that this was far more than just a legal matter. He had been a witness to a family's history being rewritten, a legacy resurrected from the ashes of time. He discreetly cleared his throat, trying to regain control of the proceedings, but it was clear that the family's reactions were anything but predictable, anything but ordinary.

The room was a cacophony of excited whispers, hushed conversations, and the occasional shriek of disbelief. Cousins, aunts, and uncles, previously unknown to Jacob, emerged from the woodwork, eager to reconnect with their newly minted billionaire relative. The air buzzed with a strange energy, a blend of joy, anxiety, and avarice. Jacob felt a wave of nausea wash over him. He couldn't help but wonder whether this newfound wealth would truly bring happiness, or whether it would only complicate the already tangled threads of his family's relationships.

The reading of the will had been a formality; the real drama, the true heart of the story, lay in the reactions of those who suddenly found their lives intertwined with Jacob's newfound fortune. It was a story of unexpected inheritance, of familial bonds tested by sudden wealth, of dreams fulfilled and lives irrevocably altered. The adventure, it seemed, was far from over. The silver dollar, nestled safe in his pocket, felt like a heavy talisman, a symbol of both incredible luck and the potentially perilous journey that lay ahead.

The world had changed in an instant, and Jacob, despite the overwhelming wealth, felt a strange sense of trepidation, a mixture of excitement and dread, as he faced the next chapter of his

extraordinary life. The implications of this inheritance were just beginning to dawn on everyone, and the fallout, it was becoming clear, would be anything but simple.

Masons Concerns

The initial euphoria began to fade, replaced by a slow, creeping unease that settled over Mason like a shroud. He'd seen the wild joy, the desperate grasping, the sudden, almost frantic shifts in family dynamics. But beneath the glittering surface of newfound wealth, he saw something far more unsettling. The sheer scale of it all was staggering, but it wasn't the billions that truly concerned him; it was the *how* .

He'd seen the way Elias and Samuel had exchanged a knowing glance, a silent acknowledgment of the secret they'd guarded for so long. He'd felt the weight of their unspoken relief, the years of hope finally bearing fruit. But that relief, Mason realized, carried a price.

A price they might not yet fully understand. Their trip through time, the meticulous retrieval of the silver dollar – it had changed the course of history, however subtly.

Mason took a deep breath, the air thick with the lingering scent of old money and nervous anticipation. He needed to speak to Jacob, needed to make sure his cousin understood the gravity of the situation. He found Jacob standing by the window, staring out at the darkening cityscape, his face a mask of bewilderment. The celebratory atmosphere had thinned, replaced by a strange quiet, punctuated only by the occasional muffled sob from Cousin Penelope, who seemed to have rediscovered a fresh supply of dramatically appropriate tears.

"Jacob," Mason said softly, his voice cutting through the muted chaos. Jacob turned, his eyes still reflecting the bewildering enormity of his newfound fortune. "We need to talk."

Jacob's face, usually alight with his characteristic optimism, was etched with lines of exhaustion and uncertainty. "About what, Mason? The... the money? Honestly, I'm still trying to wrap my head around it all." He ran a hand through his already tousled hair, a gesture that spoke volumes of his inner turmoil.

"It's not just the money, Jacob," Mason said, his voice low and serious. He pulled up a chair, settling beside his cousin, and explained, as carefully as he could, the implications of their time-travel escapade. He began with the basics, laying out the paradox of altering the past. He spoke about the butterfly effect, the unpredictable ripple that one small change could create.

"We went back in time, Jacob. We changed things. We may have inadvertently altered the course of history, even if it was just on a personal level. This inheritance...it wasn't just a fortunate discovery. It was a consequence of our actions. The silver dollar... it wasn't just a lucky find; it was a catalyst."

Jacob stared at him, his eyes wide with disbelief. "You're saying... we messed with time? That this entire thing is our fault?"

Mason nodded, a grim expression etched on his face. "We can't be certain of the full consequences. Think about it, Jacob. This fortune...it wasn't supposed to be yours. Silas Walker intended for it to go to someone else, at some other point. We changed that. We might have changed other things too, things we don't even know about yet."

He described the complexities of temporal mechanics, his explanations simplified for Jacob's comprehension, but no less alarming. He talked about potential paradoxes, about the delicate balance of time and causality. He emphasized the unpredictability of the ripple effect, painting vivid pictures of unforeseen consequences, both grand and minute.

He painted a picture of a world where, perhaps, a small, seemingly insignificant event they'd changed had caused a ripple leading to unforeseen and potentially catastrophic events. Perhaps a different person, never intended to be wealthy, experienced sudden poverty, or a family was fractured beyond repair due to unforeseen changes in their fortunes. The very fabric of time and space was, in Mason's view, incredibly fragile. And they, despite the best of intentions, had potentially torn a hole in it.

Jacob's face paled. The jovial celebratory atmosphere had completely vanished. The sheer weight of responsibility, the unforeseen consequences of their actions, now pressed down on him with crushing force. The billions seemed to shrink in significance compared to the potential consequences of their actions. The joyous relief of his family, only moments before, felt hollow and unsettling now, tinged with a nagging sense of guilt and responsibility.

"But... what can we do?" Jacob asked, his voice barely above a whisper. The weight of the situation was evident in his slumped shoulders and the drawn look on his face.

"I don't know," Mason admitted, his own unease growing. "But we need to be vigilant. We need to observe, to watch for any unexpected changes, any anomalies. We need to understand the full extent of what we've done."

He outlined a plan, suggesting a meticulous monitoring of the family's reactions, a careful analysis of their newfound wealth and how its acquisition affected them and the wider community. He suggested discreet research, a quiet examination of any potential unintended consequences. He knew that they couldn't undo what they'd done, but they could try to mitigate the damage, to limit the impact of their unintentional meddling with the timeline.

The air in the room crackled with unspoken anxieties. The joyous celebration had been replaced by a stark awareness of the potentially perilous path they'd set themselves on. The newfound wealth, once a source of exhilaration, now hung over them like a sword of Damocles, a constant reminder of the risky gamble they'd taken and the uncertain future that lay ahead.

Mason's concerns went beyond mere financial prudence. He was acutely aware of the potential for conflict, the possibility of family members turning against each other, driven by greed and ambition. He saw the seeds of discord already sown – the envious glances, the calculated smiles, the subtle hints of avarice. The newfound wealth, he knew, would test the bonds of family and loyalty to their breaking point.

He warned Jacob about the dangers of trusting blindly, advising caution and shrewdness. He pointed out the predatory nature of some of their relatives, the way they were circling Jacob like vultures, their eyes gleaming with a mixture of envy and avarice. He urged Jacob to be cautious, to proceed with measured steps, to tread carefully in this newly treacherous landscape of unimaginable wealth.

Mason, ever the pragmatist, began sketching out a plan. He spoke of setting up a team of discreet investigators, professionals who could quietly monitor any unusual activity, any ripple effects of their actions. They would need to tread carefully, to avoid drawing unwanted attention. This was not just about managing money; it was about managing a potential crisis, a temporal storm of their own making. The magnitude of their responsibility was daunting, the uncertainty of the situation deeply unsettling. The silver dollar, once a symbol of hope and adventure, now felt like a dangerous talisman, a reminder of the unforeseen consequences of their

actions. The adventure, far from being over, had just begun, and it promised to be a far more dangerous and complex journey than they'd ever imagined. The weight of the past, altered by their

hands, pressed down on them, a heavy, uncertain burden they would carry into the unpredictable future.

A New Beginning

The mahogany doors of the law firm felt heavy behind Jacob as he stepped out onto the bustling New York street. The crisp autumn air did little to cool the firestorm raging within him. Billions. The word echoed in his head, a dizzying, almost surreal concept. Billions that were his. His. The sheer weight of it threatened to crush him.

Moments ago, he'd been a struggling freelance graphic designer, barely making ends meet, living paycheck to paycheck. Now, he was a billionaire. A billionaire who knew the truth behind his sudden windfall – a truth he shared with only one other person in the world: Mason.

The celebratory atmosphere of the will reading, the hushed whispers of envy and awe, the strained smiles of long-forgotten relatives – it all felt like a distant dream, a bizarre play unfolding before him. He'd seen the avarice in their eyes, the thinly veiled calculations, the sudden, desperate attempts to ingratiate themselves into his newfound life. He saw the vultures circling, ready to pick at the carcass of his sudden fortune. Mason's words echoed in his ears: *They'll come for you, Jacob. They'll all come.*

The city, usually a source of inspiration, a canvas of vibrant energy, now felt like a suffocating cage. The towering skyscrapers, the relentless hum of traffic, the endless stream of anonymous faces – it all pressed down on him, amplifying his already overwhelming feelings. He needed to escape, to clear his head, to process the seismic shift that had occurred in his life. He needed distance, space, time to grapple with the enormity of it all.

He glanced back at the law firm, its imposing façade a stark contrast to the turmoil inside him. The grand building, a symbol of wealth and power, now represented something more complicated –a testament to a journey through time, a consequence of actions taken, a burden of responsibility far outweighing any potential joy.

He found Mason waiting for him at the curb, his face etched with the same blend of exhaustion and apprehension that Jacob felt. Mason, ever the pragmatist, had already started formulating a plan.

Their time travel escapade had thrown their lives into a chaotic orbit, and he was determined to regain control, to navigate this unpredictable new reality.

"Ready?" Mason asked, his voice low, almost a whisper.

Jacob nodded, unable to speak. The word "ready" felt utterly inappropriate. He wasn't ready. No one could be ready for such a dramatic upheaval. But he knew he couldn't stay. He couldn't face the onslaught of relatives, the vultures circling, the endless parade of lawyers and financial advisors. He needed to escape, to find a place where he could breathe, where he could begin to process the implications of what had happened.

"Let's go," Jacob finally managed, his voice raspy.

Their escape wasn't a dramatic flight; it wasn't a frantic dash away from pursuing creditors or vengeful relatives. Instead, it was a quiet retreat, a strategic withdrawal. They took a cab to Mason's

apartment, gathering a few essentials – laptops, phones, a change of clothes. Then, under the cloak of the city's twilight, they drove to JFK airport. Their destination: a small coastal town in Maine, a place Mason had visited as a child, a haven of quiet solitude.

The flight was a blur of nervous energy and subdued conversation. Jacob stared out the window, watching the sprawling cityscape shrink below, the chaos of his life receding with the distance. He thought about the changes they'd wrought – the altered timeline, the ripple effects stretching out into an uncertain future. He thought about Silas Walker, the enigmatic figure whose silver dollar had triggered this cascade of events. He thought about the potential repercussions, the unforeseen consequences that could still unfold.

The vastness of the Atlantic Ocean, spread before him, mirrored the endless possibilities, both exhilarating and terrifying, that lay ahead. The quiet hum of the aircraft, the gentle rocking motion, helped calm the whirlwind in his mind. The initial shock was starting to wear off, replaced by a creeping sense of responsibility, a heavy cloak of obligation. He carried the weight of their shared secret, the knowledge of their unintended alterations to the past, the potential risks and ramifications of their actions.

In Maine, the air was crisp and clean, a stark contrast to the thick, smoky atmosphere of New York. The small coastal town was a world away from the frantic energy of the city, a haven of tranquility and solitude. They rented a small cabin overlooking the ocean, the rhythmic crashing of the waves a soothing balm to his frayed nerves.

The cabin was simple, rustic, far removed from the opulence he'd just inherited. It was a stark reminder that material wealth was not the measure of a life well-lived. It was a space for reflection, for contemplation, a place to disentangle the complexities of his new reality. It was a refuge from the storm, a place to begin to rebuild, to find his footing in this uncharted territory.

Days turned into weeks. They worked tirelessly, sifting through financial documents, analyzing the intricacies of the inheritance. Mason's analytical skills, coupled with Jacob's creative mind, formed a formidable team. They established protocols, systems, and strategies for managing the immense wealth, ensuring its responsible and ethical deployment.

They meticulously documented everything – their time-travel experience, the implications of their actions, the potential consequences. They created a detailed log of every decision they made, every investment they pursued, every potential ripple effect they observed. They knew they were walking a tightrope, balancing the benefits of their newfound fortune with the responsibility of minimizing any potential damage.

Beyond the financial aspects, they also focused on the emotional and psychological impact of their newfound wealth. They were aware of the potential for conflict, the temptation of greed, the erosion of relationships. They established clear boundaries, safeguarding themselves from the insidious influence of avarice. They were determined to navigate this new reality with integrity, ensuring their fortune didn't corrupt them.

But beneath the methodical planning and careful execution, a deep-seated unease lingered. The weight of their secret remained, a constant reminder of their actions and their potential consequences. It was a burden they carried together, a shared responsibility that bound them closer. They were navigating uncharted waters, facing an unknown future, a future they had inadvertently shaped with a single, seemingly insignificant act. Their adventure, far from being over, had only just begun. The quiet solitude of Maine provided a much-needed respite, a space to regroup and formulate a plan. It was a new beginning, uncertain yet full of potential, a blend of triumph and uncertainty, of hope and apprehension. They were ready, to the extent that anyone could be, for the challenges that lay ahead.

The Maine coast, initially a balm to their frayed nerves, quickly lost its tranquility. The peace was shattered not by the howling wind or the crashing waves, but by a sharp rap on their cabin door. Jacob, immersed in a spreadsheet detailing their increasingly complex financial holdings, nearly jumped out of his skin. Mason, ever vigilant, was already halfway to the door, his hand instinctively reaching for the small, heavy object nestled in his pocket – a surprisingly effective pepper spray disguised as a luxury pen.

The rapping intensified, escalating from a polite knock to a forceful pounding. Mason cautiously opened the door a crack, revealing two figures silhouetted against the fading light. They were dressed in nondescript suits, their faces obscured by shadow, but their demeanor was anything but subtle. They exuded an authority that was both intimidating and unsettling. They weren't local law enforcement; this was something... different.

"Federal agents," one of them announced, his voice clipped and professional, lacking any hint of friendliness. "We need to speak to you about a matter of national security." The words hung in the air, heavy with unspoken implications.

Mason, a master of improvisation, smoothly invited them in, his mind already racing. He'd anticipated some level of scrutiny following their time-travel escapade, but he hadn't expected it to come in the form of government agents showing up at their remote Maine cabin. He knew, instinctively, that this was connected to Silas Walker's silver dollar, the catalyst for their journey through time. The implications were vast, potentially catastrophic.

Jacob, his heart pounding against his ribs, watched the agents move through their small cabin with an unnerving efficiency. They were thorough, meticulous, their eyes missing nothing. They examined their laptops, scrutinizing the carefully documented financial records, their gaze lingering on the encrypted files detailing their time-travel experiences.

"We're interested in the device," the lead agent finally stated, his tone unwavering. "The one that allowed you to... alter the timeline." The casual way he mentioned time travel sent a chill down Jacob's spine. How much did they know? How much had Silas Walker revealed?

Mason feigned ignorance; a practiced maneuver honed over years of navigating complex situations. He deflected their questions, using carefully crafted responses to buy time, to assess the situation. He needed to understand the extent of their knowledge, their capabilities, their objectives.

But their deception was short-lived. The agents, it turned out, were far from being novices. They had evidence, undeniable proof of their temporal transgression. Photographs, timelines, impossible coincidences – they held the pieces of their puzzle, and they were quickly assembling them.

The realization dawned on them with the cold certainty of a winter storm: they were not simply under investigation; they were on the run.

The ensuing chase was a blur of adrenaline and near-misses. They abandoned the cabin, leaving behind a trail of carefully placed distractions and misleading clues. They commandeered a car, weaving through the quiet coastal roads, pursued by unmarked vehicles that appeared seemingly from nowhere. The agents were relentless, their pursuit both skillful and terrifying.

They reached Portland, the city a chaotic labyrinth of streets and highways. The agents were close behind, their sirens a relentless, haunting soundtrack to their flight. They risked everything, navigating the city's frantic energy, their escape becoming a desperate dance with fate.

They lost them temporarily by taking refuge in a bustling fish market, the pungent aroma of seafood and the cacophony of shouting vendors masking their presence amidst the throngs of people. The temporary reprieve, however, was short-lived. The agents, utilizing advanced technology, quickly pinpointed their location.

Their escape continued, a breathless pursuit through alleyways, across rooftops, a chaotic ballet of evasion and pursuit. They leaped from one precarious position to another, their heartbeats echoing in the night. The city lights blurred, the sounds of their pursuers becoming an omnipresent, threatening drone.

They finally found a temporary sanctuary in an abandoned

subway station, the echoing silence a stark contrast to the frantic chase. They sat huddled together, their breaths ragged, their bodies trembling with exhaustion. The subterranean darkness provided a moment of respite, a fleeting opportunity to regroup, to formulate their next move.

The weight of their situation pressed heavily upon them. They were not simply evading the law; they were fleeing from a powerful government agency intent on retrieving a device that could alter the course of history. The stakes were impossibly high, the consequences potentially catastrophic. The seemingly insignificant act of picking up Silas Walker's silver dollar had transformed their lives in ways they couldn't have imagined.

The silence of the subway station was broken by the distant rumble of an approaching train. It was a reminder that their refuge was temporary, that their escape was far from over. The city that had once been a canvas of vibrant energy was now a relentless hunter, pursuing them with unwavering determination. The knowledge of their actions, their secret, and the consequences of their time travel was an ever-present weight, a constant reminder of their precarious position. Their journey had transformed from a sudden windfall into a high-stakes game of cat and mouse, where survival demanded quick thinking, adaptability, and a touch of sheer luck.

Their flight was a desperate attempt to reclaim control, to navigate the chaotic consequences of their actions. The simple act of finding a safe place to sleep became a high-stakes mission. The sounds of the city, once inspiring, now held a sinister undertone, each siren a reminder of their perilous position. Their adventure was no longer a simple story of inherited wealth; it was a fight for survival against a formidable opponent.

They knew they couldn't stay hidden forever. They needed a plan, a strategy to outwit their pursuers, a way to evade their relentless pursuit. They needed to understand their motives, to anticipate their next move, to regain control of the situation. The escape from the Maine cabin marked the beginning of a new, far more dangerous chapter in their lives, a chapter where the stakes were exponentially higher. The quiet solitude of Maine was a distant memory, replaced by the constant threat of capture, the shadow of pursuit looming over their every move.

They spent hours poring over maps, studying escape routes, and devising elaborate plans of deception, all fueled by adrenaline and fueled by a grim determination to survive. Their escape was less a flight and more a carefully orchestrated series of calculated maneuvers, a game of chess played with the very fabric of their lives as the stakes. They knew their time was limited; the longer they remained on the run, the greater the chance of capture. The city, once a source of inspiration, now felt like a hostile entity, a maze of endless possibilities for both escape and capture.

The quiet, carefully planned retreat from Maine had morphed into a full-blown, desperate flight for survival, a high-stakes chase across the urban landscape. Their newfound wealth, once a source of overwhelming joy and anxiety, was now a liability, a beacon drawing their pursuers closer. They were trapped in a game of their own making, a game with no clear rules, no defined boundaries, and no guarantees of survival. The adventure had taken on a new dimension, a far more dangerous and unpredictable path. The fight for survival had begun, and their only goal was to make it out alive.

The abandoned subway station offered little in the way of comfort, but it offered respite. The echoing silence was a stark contrast to the cacophony of the chase, the damp air a chilling reminder of their precarious situation. Jacob, his breath ragged, leaned against a cold, damp pillar, his fingers tracing the worn graffiti on the wall. Mason, ever the pragmatist, was already rummaging through their meager belongings, a small flashlight illuminating his face, its beam dancing across the scattered maps and half-eaten energy bars.

"We can't stay here," Mason said, his voice low and urgent. "They'll find us."

Jacob nodded; his gaze fixed on the tracks disappearing into the darkness. The rumble of an approaching train had been a stark warning; their sanctuary was temporary. He pulled out his phone, the screen illuminating his pale face. No signal. Of course.

"We need a plan," Jacob said, his voice tight with anxiety. "A real plan, not just running blind."

Their previous escapes had been improvisational, fueled by adrenaline and a healthy dose of luck. This time, they needed strategy, something more calculated, more... sustainable. They needed to anticipate their pursuers' moves, to think like them, to outsmart them.

Mason, always the strategist, started outlining their options. He began by analyzing their pursuers. These weren't just any federal agents; their efficiency, their technology, their knowledge of their time-travel escapade hinted at something larger, something more sinister. They were clearly well-funded, well-equipped, and incredibly resourceful.

"They know about the device," Mason stated, his voice laced with a grim determination. "That means Silas Walker talked. The question is, how much did he tell them?"

That question hung heavy in the air, the silence of the subway station amplifying its weight. The implications were chilling. If the government knew about the device – the temporal displacement device – the implications extended far beyond their own predicament. This wasn't just about a chase; this was about control, about the potential disruption of history itself. The stakes had escalated exponentially.

They spent the next few hours poring over maps, plotting escape routes, considering various scenarios. Their options were limited, each fraught with peril. They considered fleeing the city altogether, perhaps heading north, towards Canada. But that would require transportation, and any noticeable movement would surely attract attention.

They discussed the possibility of disguises, of blending in, of becoming invisible. But they knew, realistically, their chances of slipping through the net of surveillance were minimal. The government agency pursuing them clearly possessed advanced technology, technology capable of tracking them even amidst the urban chaos.

Their discussion was punctuated by the sporadic rumbling of passing trains, each echoing the urgency of their situation. The abandoned station, once a refuge, now felt like a cage, its walls closing in.

As dawn broke, painting the sky with hues of gray and orange, they made a decision. They couldn't outrun their pursuers indefinitely. They needed to outsmart them, to exploit a weakness, to turn the tables.

Their plan was audacious, borderline insane, but it was their only hope. They would use their knowledge of the city – the city that had become their relentless hunter – against its pursuers. They would leverage its very complexity, its anonymity, its energy to disappear into the crowd, to become indistinguishable from the millions of others navigating its chaotic streets.

Their first step was to acquire new identities, new faces, new everything. They used their newfound wealth, their once-liability, to access a network of underground contacts. Contacts who could provide them with false documents, new disguises, and safe houses, hidden amongst the city's labyrinthine underbelly.

The transformation was remarkable. Jacob, with his usually neatly-groomed hair and tailored suits, became a grizzled construction worker, his face obscured by a thick beard and a worn hard hat. Mason, his impeccably dressed appearance replaced by the attire of a street artist, his face subtly altered with makeup and a carefully cultivated persona.

Their new identities were not just costumes; they were strategies, carefully designed to blend into their surroundings. They spent days immersed in their new roles, learning the nuances of their adopted personas, absorbing the rhythms of their environments.

The chase continued, but it was now a different kind of chase, a more subtle, more strategic game of cat and mouse. They moved through the city like shadows, using the cover of anonymity to their advantage, always one step ahead of their pursuers. They employed a network of safe houses, constantly shifting locations, leaving no trace.

They utilized their knowledge of history, of urban geography, to their advantage, navigating the city's hidden passages, its forgotten corners, its undercurrents. They exploited the city's anonymity, its relentless energy, its ability to both conceal and expose.

The government agency, accustomed to high-tech surveillance, was ill-prepared for this change in tactics. Their sophisticated technology was useless against two men who were not just fleeing but actively shaping their environment, molding themselves to the city's contours, becoming one with the urban fabric.

Their escape became a test of endurance, of intellect, of cunning. It was a battle of wits, a dance with fate, a relentless pursuit

through the heart of a city transformed into both their hunter and their shield. The city, once a symbol of their relentless pursuit, now became an unlikely ally, a silent conspirator in their desperate fight for survival.

The days blurred into weeks, the pursuit becoming a relentless, nerve-wracking routine of escapes, near misses, and carefully planned maneuvers. But as weeks turned into months, the pursuit began to lose its intensity. The federal agents, frustrated by their inability to track the two men, slowly but surely, began to lose ground. Their sophisticated technology was no match for the cunning and adaptability of their targets.

The weight of their actions still weighed heavily on them, but the constant threat of capture began to subside. The fear didn't disappear, but it was replaced by a growing determination, a shared resolve to outwit their pursuers and reclaim their lives from the clutches of a shadowy government agency. Their escape from the Maine cabin had been just the beginning. This, the life of evasion and calculated strategy amidst the chaotic urban sprawl, was a far more complex, challenging, and ultimately, rewarding test of resilience. Their journey into the unknown had transformed them, forged their resilience in the fires of pursuit. They emerged, not unscathed, but strengthened. Their adventure was far from over, but for now, they had won a crucial battle in the war for their survival.

Their initial success in evading the relentless pursuit of the federal agents was a fragile victory. The city, their unlikely ally, had provided cover, but it couldn't offer lasting protection. They needed more than just anonymity; they needed allies, and those allies were proving harder to find than they anticipated. Their resources, while substantial, were dwindling. The money pilfered from Silas Walker's ill-gotten gains, once a lifeline, was slowly being depleted. They were living on borrowed time, and the clock was ticking.

One rain-lashed evening, huddled in a cramped, dimly lit apartment above a bustling Chinatown restaurant, their usual quiet strategizing was interrupted by a frantic knock on the door. Jacob, disguised as a wiry, bespectacled librarian, peered through the peephole, his heart pounding in his chest. He recognized the face; it belonged to a woman, her eyes glittering with a wild energy, a street artist whose work they'd encountered several times over the past few months. Her name, they learned later, was Anya Petrova.

Anya, her vibrant purple hair plastered to her forehead by the relentless rain, burst in, breathless and energized. "You're the time travelers," she announced, her voice hushed but insistent. "The ones they're hunting." She didn't need an introduction. Word travels fast in the city's underbelly, especially when it involves government conspiracies and time travel.

Behind her, two more figures emerged from the shadows: a towering man with a shock of white hair and an unnervingly calm demeanor, and a young woman with a mischievous grin and eyes that sparkled with intelligence. The man introduced himself as Professor Eldridge, a retired astrophysicist with a reputation for unorthodox theories and even more unorthodox experiments. The woman, a tech whiz named Kai, was Eldridge's protege, her fingers constantly tapping at a battered laptop.

"We've been watching you," Professor Eldridge continued, his voice calm and measured. "Your methods are... impressive. But you're running out of time."

Their initial reaction was suspicion. Why would these strangers, seemingly plucked from the city's eccentric fringe, risk aiding them? But Anya quickly dispelled their doubts. "We have a vested interest in keeping that device out of NASA's hands," she explained, gesturing vaguely. "It's not just about you anymore; it's

about preventing a catastrophic misuse of temporal technology."

Their skepticism melted away as Eldridge and Kai laid out their case. They weren't just eccentrics; they were members of a clandestine group called the Chrononauts, a ragtag collective dedicated to safeguarding temporal technology from those who would misuse it. They'd been tracking the time-travel device since its inception, aware of its potential to rewrite history, to unleash chaos upon the world. They had learned about Jacob and Mason's escape, their abilities, and their desperate flight. They needed their help.

"NASA," Eldridge explained, "is not what you think it is. There's a shadow organization within, a group hell-bent on exploiting the device for their own nefarious ends. They've already tried to take it for themselves, multiple times."

Kai chimed in, her fingers flying across her laptop keyboard. "We've intercepted their communications. They're planning to use the device to alter historical events to solidify their power. We've traced some of the key figures involved: individuals with connections to some of the most powerful corporations. It's a sprawling network of corruption."

The Chrononauts, they learned, were a diverse group. Their motives, while unified in their desire to protect the timeline, were incredibly varied. Anya, a street artist with a burning passion for justice, sought to expose the corrupt organizations that threatened the fabric of society. Professor Eldridge, a scientist disillusioned by the misuse of scientific advancement, sought to prevent a cataclysmic alteration of history. Kai, fueled by a restless curiosity and a desire to challenge authority, craved the intellectual thrill of the chase. This unlikely alliance was formed not out of shared ideals alone, but out of a mutual understanding of the stakes involved.

The Chrononauts had resources and skills that Jacob and Mason desperately needed. They provided them with access to secure communication channels, advanced technology to evade surveillance, and a network of safe houses extending far beyond the confines of their city. In return, Jacob and Mason offered their unique understanding of the device and their unparalleled ability to elude the federal agents. It was a perfect, though precarious, symbiosis.

The ensuing weeks were a blur of clandestine meetings, daring escapes, and intricate strategies. They uncovered a network of corruption reaching the highest echelons of power. The agents pursuing them were merely pawns in a larger game, puppets dancing to the tune of a shadowy organization pulling the strings from the background. With the Chrononauts' help, Jacob and Mason not only evaded capture but started to fight back.

They used their knowledge of the city's underbelly, coupled with the Chrononauts' technological prowess, to disrupt the shadow organization's operations. They planted false information, leaked sensitive data, and generally sowed chaos within their ranks. Anya's artistry proved invaluable in creating elaborate distractions, diverting attention and confusing their pursuers. Professor Eldridge's knowledge of physics and temporal mechanics provided critical insights into the device's capabilities, enabling them to anticipate the shadow organization's next move. And Kai, with her hacking skills, became their eyes and ears, piercing through layers of digital security to expose the organization's secrets.

Their collaboration wasn't always smooth. The Chrononauts, each with their own eccentricities and conflicting approaches, often clashed. Anya's impulsive nature sometimes clashed with Eldridge's meticulous planning, while Kai's technological prowess occasionally threatened to overshadow their more human-based strategies. But amidst the clashes and disagreements, a powerful

sense of camaraderie developed, a bond forged in the crucible of shared adversity and a common goal.

One evening, huddled together in a hidden bunker deep beneath the city, they reviewed their progress. The initial panic of the chase had been replaced by a quiet determination, a shared sense of purpose that transcended their individual backgrounds. They were no longer just two men on the run; they were part of a movement, a resistance against the forces that threatened to alter the very fabric of time. The city, once their hunting ground, had become their base of operations, its chaotic energy fueling their fight for survival.

Their fight, however, was far from over. The shadow organization, stung by their recent setbacks, was regrouping, preparing for a final showdown. Their unexpected alliance had given them a fighting chance, but the stakes remained incredibly high. The future of time itself hung in the balance, and the fate of the world rested on the shoulders of this unlikely band of heroes. Their journey had taken them from a quiet Maine cabin to the chaotic heart of a city teeming with secrets, and the adventure was only just beginning. The next phase of their fight would demand everything they had: their cunning, their skills, and most importantly, their unwavering resolve to protect the integrity of time. The fight for survival had evolved into a battle for the future. The hum of the device, usually a steady, reassuring thrum, had become erratic, a frantic buzzing that vibrated through the floor of the Chrononauts' hidden bunker. Red lights pulsed erratically on its sleek, obsidian surface, a stark contrast to its usual cool, almost elegant aesthetic. Jacob, his brow furrowed in concentration, ran a hand over the smooth casing, his fingers tracing the intricate circuitry visible beneath the transparent panel.

"It's unstable," he murmured, his voice barely audible above the machine's increasingly agitated whine. "The temporal flux is fluctuating wildly."

Mason, ever the pragmatist, checked their emergency power supply. "How much longer before it completely fries itself?"

Kai, her fingers dancing across her laptop, frowned. "The energy signature is spiking. It's drawing power at an unsustainable rate. Whatever's causing this, it's overwhelming the internal regulators."

Professor Eldridge, usually the picture of calm composure, paced restlessly. "The chronometric stabilizer... it's failing. The initial design was flawed, I admit. We pushed the boundaries of temporal mechanics. We underestimated the complexities of manipulating spacetime on this scale." He ran a hand through his already chaotic white hair, his voice tinged with self-reproach. "My calculations were... optimistic, to say the least."

The problem, they soon discovered, wasn't just a simple power surge. The device, in its desperate attempt to maintain temporal coherence, was drawing energy from unexpected sources. It was siphoning power from the bunker's emergency generators, causing lights to flicker and alarms to blare. It was even drawing energy from the surrounding environment, causing minor electromagnetic disturbances that sent Kai's laptop into a frenzy of error messages.

"It's like it's trying to... borrow time from somewhere else," Anya offered, her usual ebullient energy replaced by a serious intensity. "Like it's creating a temporal debt."

The implications were terrifying. The device wasn't just malfunctioning; it was potentially creating temporal paradoxes, rifts in the fabric of spacetime. A localized temporal anomaly could manifest as anything from a brief distortion of reality to a catastrophic disruption of the timeline. And given the unpredictable nature of the device, the consequences were impossible to predict.

The immediate challenge was to stabilize the device before it caused irreversible damage, both to itself and potentially to the world around them. But the device's internal systems were too complex for even Kai's considerable technological prowess to decipher quickly. The intricate network of quantum processors, chronometric stabilizers, and temporal regulators was a bewildering labyrinth of microchips and wires. It was a symphony of cutting-edge science, and right now, that symphony was playing a chaotic dissonant chord.

"We need to bypass the failing chronometric stabilizer," Eldridge announced, his voice regaining some of its composure. "We need to find a way to manually control the temporal flux." He sketched a complex diagram on a whiteboard, his hand moving with surprising speed. "It involves recalibrating the quantum entanglement matrix, adjusting the temporal displacement parameters, and..." he trailed off, lost in the intricate details of his own calculations.

The next few hours were a blur of frantic activity. Kai, despite the limitations of her equipment, managed to secure a temporary connection to a powerful university server, providing them with access to a vast database of scientific papers and research data. Eldridge, poring over the information, mumbled equations and whispered cryptic pronouncements about quantum entanglement and spacetime curvature. Jacob and Mason, guided by Eldridge's calculations and Kai's technical expertise, worked tirelessly to modify the device's internal circuitry. Anya, ever practical, coordinated their efforts, ensuring they had the tools and materials they needed.

They faced numerous setbacks. Several attempts to recalibrate the quantum entanglement matrix failed, each time causing the device to generate an even more erratic energy signature. The temporal displacement parameters proved incredibly sensitive, with even minor adjustments resulting in significant fluctuations in the temporal flux. The task was akin to defusing a bomb while simultaneously trying to understand its intricate mechanism. One wrong move and the consequences could be catastrophic.

Finally, after what seemed like an eternity of stressful work, a breakthrough occurred. Kai discovered a hidden subroutine within the device's software, a failsafe protocol designed to stabilize the system in emergency situations. It was a last resort, a brute-force method that risked overloading the device, but it was their only hope.

With a shared glance of grim determination, they activated the failsafe protocol. The device's erratic buzzing momentarily ceased, replaced by a low hum that slowly increased in intensity. The red lights on its surface gradually shifted to a steady green, a small victory in the midst of their struggle.

However, their triumph was short-lived. As the device stabilized, a new problem emerged: the failsafe protocol had created a side effect they hadn't anticipated. The device's temporal displacement capabilities had been amplified, but its accuracy had been compromised. Their next jump could send them anywhere, anytime – a terrifying prospect, considering they were already being hunted by a powerful and ruthless organization.

The device, they realized, was now more unpredictable than ever before. Their escape from the federal agents, their alliance with the Chrononauts, their seemingly steady progress against the shadow organization – all of it could be jeopardized by a single, uncontrollable jump. The technological challenges had shifted from stabilizing the device to mitigating the dangers of its enhanced, albeit erratic, capabilities. The fight for survival had now become a race against time and the unpredictable forces of temporal mechanics. They were running against the clock, and the clock, it seemed, was ticking in reverse.

The Chrononauts' modified van, a battered relic of a bygone era now repurposed for time travel, lurched violently, throwing them against their restraints. The world outside dissolved into a kaleidoscope of swirling colors and fractured images, a chaotic ballet of light and shadow that left them disoriented and breathless. When the jarring sensation finally subsided, they found themselves in a place utterly unlike anything they had ever seen.

Gone was the sterile, metallic interior of their bunker. Instead, they were surrounded by the earthy scent of damp soil and the echoing drip of water. The van rested in a cavernous space, bathed in the soft, ethereal glow of bioluminescent fungi that clung to the damp walls. The air hung heavy with the smell of ozone and something else, something subtly sweet and oddly familiar.

"Where... where are we?" Anya gasped, her voice still shaky from the jarring jump. Her usually vibrant eyes were wide with a mixture of awe and apprehension.

Jacob, ever the cautious one, cautiously unbuckled his restraints. He grabbed his pulse rifle, its weight reassuring in his hand. "It seems our failsafe didn't quite work as planned," he muttered, his gaze sweeping across the vast subterranean chamber.

Mason, ever practical, was already examining the van's instruments. "The temporal coordinates are... meaningless. We're outside the known parameters of our time stream. This isn't just a geographical location; it's a whole other dimension."

Professor Eldridge, his face pale but his eyes gleaming with intellectual excitement, approached a wall pulsating with a gentle, rhythmic light. He touched it, and the wall shimmered, revealing a hidden passage leading deeper into the earth. "This," he whispered, his voice trembling with a mixture of wonder and apprehension, "is extraordinary. This is... a hidden city."

The passage led them to a sprawling network of tunnels and caverns, illuminated by a similar bioluminescent flora. They walked past massive chambers carved from the rock, each decorated with intricate murals depicting scenes of an unknown history. The figures in the paintings were humanoid, but not quite human, with elongated limbs and large, expressive eyes. The murals depicted advanced technology, flying machines, and cities that seemed to float amidst the clouds. It felt like stepping into a lost civilization, a testament to a forgotten age.

They eventually reached a larger cavern, a vast space bathed in the soft glow of the fungi. In the center of the cavern, a city had been built. Structures of polished obsidian and shimmering crystal rose from the earth, their smooth surfaces reflecting the light in dazzling displays. Buildings twisted and turned in an organic fashion, following the contours of the cavern walls, creating a stunning and surreal cityscape. The sounds of a thriving civilization reached them - the murmur of voices, the rhythmic clang of metal on metal, the low hum of some unknown technology.

As they approached the city, cautiously making their way through the intricate network of tunnels and walkways, they began to encounter its inhabitants. They were humanoid, yet their appearance defied easy categorization. Some were tall and slender, with skin that shimmered like polished jade. Others were shorter, their bodies thick and muscular, with skin that resembled polished ebony. Yet despite their physical differences, they shared a certain grace and elegance in their movements. Their eyes, large and luminous, held an ancient wisdom, a depth that spoke of untold centuries.

Initially, the inhabitants observed the Chrononauts from a

distance, their expressions unreadable. There was no overt hostility, but neither was there any welcome. It was as if they were apparitions, ghosts from another time, suddenly materialized in their midst. After a tense period of observation, a group of the jade-skinned beings approached, their movements fluid and graceful. They gestured for the Chrononauts to follow them, communicating through a series of silent, almost hypnotic movements.

They were led to a central plaza, a vast space where the city's inhabitants gathered. At the center of the plaza stood a colossal structure of obsidian, its surface covered in intricate carvings that seemed to writhe and shift in the soft light. The structure pulsed with a faint energy, a low hum that resonated through the entire cavern.

They were brought before a council of elders, their faces etched with the wisdom of ages. The elders, unlike the other inhabitants, appeared truly ancient, their bodies frail yet radiating an immense power. They communicated through a series of telepathic images, showing the Chrononauts scenes of their history, their struggles, their triumphs, and their deep connection to the earth.

The Chrononauts learned that this underground city, known as "Terra", was not a hidden civilization in the traditional sense, but a refuge—a sanctuary shielded from the ravages of time and the conflicts of the surface world. They were not simply survivors, but guardians, keepers of ancient knowledge and technologies lost to the surface dwellers for millennia. Their city was powered by a natural energy source, a geothermal vent that provided them with nearly limitless energy. They lived in harmony with the earth, using its resources sustainably and responsibly.

However, their peaceful existence was not without its threats. The elders revealed that their existence was a closely guarded secret.

They had been forced underground centuries ago to escape a cataclysmic war, a conflict of unimaginable scale and devastation that had scarred the surface world. The technology of Terra, although advanced, was intentionally kept hidden, for the elders feared the consequences if their inventions fell into the wrong hands.

The council explained that their advanced technology was not meant for aggression, but for the preservation of life and the balance of nature. They had developed methods to heal the earth, to cleanse the environment of pollution, and to create sustainable sources of energy. But they remained cautious, choosing to remain hidden until the surface world was ready to embrace a future of peace and harmony.

They learned that the strange sweet smell permeating the air was a byproduct of the Terra's unique energy source—a subtle, almost imperceptible aroma of ancient earth and blooming life. It was a constant reminder of their connection to the planet and the delicate balance they strived to maintain.

The council also revealed their suspicions regarding the shadow organization hunting the Chrononauts. They sensed the organization's malevolent presence, the disturbance in the temporal fabric, the disruption to the natural order. They recognized the inherent danger the organization posed, not only to the Chrononauts but to the very fabric of time itself. Their existence was not only about preserving their own society, but protecting the balance of all timelines.

The council offered the Chrononauts a choice: remain in Terra and aid in their mission to preserve and heal the surface world, or continue their escape, carrying with them the knowledge of Terra's existence and the burden of its secrets. This decision would determine not only the fate of the Chrononauts but also the future of a world that remained unaware of the civilization hidden deep beneath its surface. The weight of this choice rested heavily upon them. Their journey, already fraught with danger, was about to become even more complex, weaving together the threads of time, secrets, and a desperate fight for survival. The clock was still ticking, but now it ticked in a far more profound and mysterious way.

The council's telepathic communication faded, leaving the Chrononauts suspended in a silence heavier than the subterranean air. The weight of their newfound knowledge pressed down on them, a crushing burden of secrets and possibilities. Professor Eldridge, usually so voluble, was speechless, his gaze fixed on the obsidian structure pulsating softly in the center of the plaza. Anya, her initial awe tempered by a dawning apprehension, nervously fingered the worn leather strap of her satchel. Only Mason, ever the pragmatist, seemed to be processing the information with his usual detached efficiency.

"So," he began, his voice low, "the failsafe... it wasn't a malfunction. It was... directed."

Jacob, still clutching his pulse rifle, nodded slowly. The council's revelations had painted a far more sinister picture than any simple equipment failure. The organization hunting them wasn't just some random group of rogue time travelers. They were far more powerful, far more organized, and their motives extended beyond simple theft or destruction. Their actions seemed designed to destabilize the very fabric of time itself. And his great-uncle, the enigmatic inventor of the Chrononaut device, somehow seemed to be entangled in this intricate web.

"My great-uncle... Elias Thorne," Jacob murmured, the name tasting like ash in his mouth. He'd always viewed his great-uncle as a brilliant, eccentric inventor, a man consumed by his work, lost in a world of gears and equations. But the council's subtle hints had painted a very different portrait – a man who held secrets far deeper than any technological innovation. A man who might have been instrumental in both creating the Chrononaut device and creating the very vulnerability that the organization was exploiting.

Mason, ever the detective, began to piece together the clues. He'd spent days poring over Elias Thorne's scant writings, blueprints, and scattered notes left behind in his dusty laboratory. They were filled with cryptic equations, half-finished schematics, and bizarre symbols that seemed to defy logical explanation. He'd dismissed them as the ramblings of a brilliant mind teetering on the brink of madness. But now, in the light of the council's revelations, they seemed to hold a sinister, hidden meaning.

"Elias's notes," Mason said, his voice taking on a new intensity. "They're not just random scribbles. They're a cipher. A complex code, built around the very principles of temporal mechanics. And the key to deciphering it... it might be embedded within the Chrononaut device itself."

Jacob felt a chill run down his spine. The implications were staggering. If the organization had access to Elias's notes, if they understood the device's inner workings better than he did, then their pursuit wasn't just about capturing the Chrononauts – it was about controlling the technology, about wielding the power to manipulate time itself.

"But why?" Anya asked, her voice laced with a mixture of fear and fascination. "What could they possibly want with the ability to travel through time?"

The council's images flashed through Jacob's mind: scenes of unimaginable destruction, global conflicts, a world scarred and ravaged by war. He had glimpsed the potential for catastrophic misuse, a power capable of rewriting history itself. The organization wasn't interested in simply changing the past; they were trying to erase it, to create a future under their absolute control.

Mason continued his analysis, running his fingers over the worn control panel of the Chrononaut van. He discovered a hidden compartment, concealed beneath a seemingly innocuous panel. Inside, he found a small, intricately engraved metal disc. The disc was covered in symbols that mirrored those in Elias Thorne's notes.

"This," Mason whispered, his eyes wide with excitement and apprehension, "This is the key."

The disc, when activated, revealed a hidden sequence of controls, a series of adjustments that had been locked away since the device's creation. It seemed Elias had anticipated this possibility, creating a failsafe mechanism hidden within the heart of his invention. It was a masterstroke of design, a precaution taken to ensure the technology wouldn't fall into the wrong hands. The sequence was designed to disrupt the device's temporal stability, making it impossible for any outsider to use it. But it had a secondary function, too. The disc could pinpoint the origins of the temporal distortions—the precise moment in time when the organization's interference began.

With trepidation and exhilaration swirling within him, Jacob activated the sequence. The Chrononaut van shuddered, the air crackling with energy. The temporal coordinates stabilized, then shifted. A new set of numbers flashed on the console: a specific date and location, far removed from their current predicament. It was a date before Elias Thorne's death, a date that placed them at the very heart of the conspiracy.

The council of Terra, sensing the shift in the temporal currents, projected images of their past, now overlaid with glimpses of Elias Thorne's work. They confirmed that Elias hadn't been working alone. He'd been in contact with members of the organization, but there was evidence that he'd been trying to thwart their plans, to counteract their influence. He'd been working on a counter-measure, a way to safeguard the device and prevent its misuse, even if it meant sacrificing his own life. The hidden compartment, the encoded disc—these were his last attempts at self-preservation, at protecting the very fabric of time itself.

The organization, it turned out, hadn't just wanted to steal the Chrononaut device; they'd sought to exploit it to rewrite history itself. They were attempting to erase certain events, to alter the very course of human civilization. Elias Thorne had discovered their plot and decided to take action. His invention became a tool not only for exploration but for protection. He created the failsafe, the hidden mechanism that the Chrononauts had stumbled upon. His death, previously believed to be accidental, had now become a tragic sacrifice, a last-ditch attempt to prevent a temporal apocalypse.

The newfound information revealed a shocking truth: Elias Thorne wasn't just a brilliant inventor; he was a reluctant hero, a defender of the timeline, his work far more profound than anyone had imagined. The Chrononauts, far from being mere time travelers, were now the inheritors of his legacy, thrust into the role of guardians, entrusted with a responsibility far greater than they could have ever anticipated. Their journey wasn't just about surviving; it was about protecting the integrity of time itself. The clock was still ticking, and they were running out of time.

The Chrononaut van hummed, a low thrumming that vibrated through Jacob's bones. The coordinates, a date nearly a century in the past, pulsed on the console – 1923, Chicago. The air crackled with anticipation, a mixture of fear and exhilaration that tightened his stomach into a knot. Anya stared out the window, her usual bright eyes shadowed with concern. Mason, ever the meticulous scientist, ran final checks on the temporal stabilizer, his fingers dancing across the control panel with practiced ease.

The jump was smoother than anticipated. One moment they were in the sterile, metallic interior of the Chrononaut, the next they found themselves in a bustling Chicago street, the air thick with the scent of coal smoke and freshly baked bread. The buildings were a blend of Art Deco elegance and the grittier realities of the Roaring Twenties, a stark contrast to the technologically advanced world they had left behind.

Their destination, according to the encoded disc, was a hidden community nestled within the city's underbelly – a haven for temporal anomalies, a secret society that had existed for centuries, safeguarding knowledge and technology far beyond their time. The disc's instructions led them to a seemingly innocuous speakeasy, its exterior masking a labyrinthine network of tunnels and hidden chambers.

The speakeasy, called "The Chronos Club," was a paradox of its time. Jazz music spilled onto the street, mingling with the raucous laughter of patrons enjoying illicit cocktails. But behind a hidden bookcase, a secret passage revealed a world untouched by the passage of time. The air inside was cool and damp, the walls lined with shelves overflowing with ancient texts and technological marvels that defied explanation.

It was here, amidst the hushed whispers and flickering candlelight, that they began to unravel the mystery of Elias Thorne. They found records, journals, and blueprints detailing his experiments with temporal mechanics, his obsession with pushing the boundaries of time itself. But more importantly, they discovered his connection to the organization hunting them – a shadowy group known only as "The Architects."

Through a series of fragmented holographic projections, they saw Elias Thorne, young and ambitious, initially collaborating with The Architects. He was fascinated by their knowledge of temporal physics, eager to learn from their mastery of time manipulation.

But over time, as he delved deeper into their research, he uncovered their true intentions – not simply to control time, but to rewrite it, to reshape history to fit their warped vision of a perfect world.

The projections revealed a growing chasm between Elias and The Architects. He grew increasingly uneasy with their methods, their disregard for the potential consequences of altering the past. He saw the devastation they could unleash, the chaos they could create. He tried to warn them, to dissuade them from their reckless pursuit of power. But they were unyielding, their ambition blinding them to the potential for catastrophe.

Elias's attempts at reasoning fell on deaf ears. The Architects saw him as a threat, a loose end that needed to be silenced. They turned against him, attempting to seize his research, to claim his invention for their own. Elias, realizing the danger, went underground, using his knowledge of temporal mechanics to create a failsafe – a hidden mechanism within the Chrononaut, designed to thwart The Architects' plans and protect the integrity of the timeline.

The hidden community, it turned out, was Elias's refuge, a network of allies who shared his concerns and helped him conceal his invention, to protect the future from The Architects' machinations. They had hidden the truth about his death, concealing the circumstances to protect their secret. His death, initially believed an accident, was carefully orchestrated by The Architects, a means of silencing their greatest adversary. They had planted the false narrative of an accidental death to avoid the unwanted attention that might follow the discovery of Elias Thorne's disappearance.

Within the community's archives, they found countless examples of Elias's ingenuity: miniature time-traveling devices, experimental energy sources, and intricate designs of alternate realities. His notes, once dismissed as the ramblings of a madman, now revealed themselves as brilliant, if eccentric, solutions to complex temporal paradoxes. They uncovered his detailed studies of temporal anomalies, his relentless pursuit of understanding the universe's intricate workings. One particular set of notes, written in a cryptic code, described a method for predicting and counteracting temporal distortions – the very distortions caused by The Architects.

They also found evidence of Elias's ongoing communication with other temporal researchers, scientists scattered across different eras, who had been warned about the Architect's plans. Elias had created a clandestine network, a silent rebellion against the Architects, fighting from the shadows to preserve the integrity of history. It was a web of interconnected timelines, a silent defense against a threat that spanned centuries. He'd anticipated his eventual betrayal and subsequent assassination, ensuring that his work wouldn't be easily seized. The Chrononaut, the hidden compartment and the encoded disc were all part of a larger plan, a cunning strategy to keep the technology from falling into the wrong hands.

The archival records contained detailed blueprints for an anti-temporal distortion device, a machine capable of neutralizing the effects of the Architects' time-altering technology. The device was incomplete, a testament to the urgency of Elias's work and the limited time he had before his betrayal. The materials required were scattered across different eras, some still inaccessible to the Chrononauts.

As Jacob pored over the documents, a profound sadness washed over him. He'd always viewed his great-uncle as an eccentric inventor, a distant figure lost in his own world of gears and equations. Now, he saw a courageous and selfless man, a visionary who had sacrificed his life to protect the world from a catastrophic threat. His great-uncle's legacy extended far beyond his inventions; he was a protector, a silent guardian of the timeline.

The weight of his great-uncle's sacrifice settled heavily upon Jacob's shoulders. He was no longer just a time traveler on a mission to survive; he was the inheritor of Elias Thorne's legacy, tasked with completing his unfinished work, with protecting the future from The Architects' designs. The burden was immense, but so was the resolve that ignited within him. He was ready to fight. He would not let his great-uncle's sacrifice be in vain. The clock was ticking, but the game had just begun. The hunt for the missing components of the anti-temporal distortion device would begin immediately, and the Chrononauts were fully committed to the task ahead. The fight to preserve the integrity of time itself was on.

The air in the Chronos Club's hidden chamber crackled with a tension far more potent than the static electricity humming from the ancient machinery lining the walls. The discovery of Elias Thorne's sacrifice, his desperate fight against The Architects, had fueled a burning determination within the Chrononauts, but it also cast a long shadow of foreboding. They weren't just chasing a device; they were playing a deadly game against an enemy with centuries of experience and seemingly limitless resources.

Mason, ever the pragmatist, began meticulously cataloging the remaining blueprints for the anti-temporal distortion device. The schematics were intricate, a labyrinthine web of equations and diagrams that defied easy comprehension. He pointed to a section marked with a faded red X. "This component," he explained, his voice low, "is the keystone. Without it, the device is useless. The annotations suggest it requires a specific type of rare earth element, found only in a collapsed mine in the Siberian tundra in 1908."

Anya, ever the strategist, leaned forward, her fingers tracing the faded lines on the blueprint. "1908," she murmured. "That's...

problematic. The Tunguska event. The area is still highly unstable, riddled with unpredictable temporal anomalies. We risk getting caught in a temporal vortex, or worse, altering the event itself." The implications hung heavy in the air – even a minor alteration could cause catastrophic ripples throughout history.

Jacob, his mind still reeling from the revelation of his great-uncle's heroism, felt the weight of responsibility pressing down on him. He had inherited not only his uncle's legacy, but also his dangerous enemies. "We have to find it," he stated, his voice firm despite the tremor of fear that ran through him. "The Architects won't stop until they have the device. If they succeed, who knows what they'll do to the timeline?"

The idea of The Architects controlling the flow of time sent shivers down his spine. The implications were terrifying, a world reshaped to fit their twisted vision, a world where the very fabric of reality could be unravelled at their whim. The stakes were impossibly high; failure wasn't simply an option; it was annihilation.

Their journey to Siberia was fraught with peril. The Chrononaut, despite its advanced technology, was not impervious to the unpredictable forces of time. The jump to 1908 was harrowing, a chaotic tumble through swirling vortexes of light and sound. They emerged near the collapsed mine, the landscape ravaged and eerily silent, the air heavy with the lingering residue of immense energy. The surrounding forest displayed the telltale signs of the Tunguska event - flattened trees extending for miles, radiating from a central point. The scene evoked a palpable sense of devastation.

The mine itself was a treacherous labyrinth, its tunnels unstable and prone to collapse. The temporal anomalies were even more unpredictable than Anya had anticipated. Flickering shadows danced in their peripheral vision, the ground trembled beneath their feet, and whispers of voices, both human and inhuman, echoed through the darkness. They navigated the mine with Mason's careful guidance, his scientific instruments constantly scanning for temporal distortions and warning them of impending danger.

Their progress was constantly interrupted by unexpected shifts in time, moments when the past momentarily bled into the present. They encountered fleeting glimpses of the event itself - a blinding flash of light, a deafening roar, the earth quaking violently beneath them. These were not mere hallucinations; they were tangible encounters with the unpredictable nature of the time-stream.

Their biggest challenge, however, wasn't the unstable environment, but the Architects' relentless pursuit. They weren't simply monitoring the Chrononauts' movements; they were actively hunting them. Throughout their expedition, they found evidence of the Architects' presence - subtle alterations to the landscape, cryptic messages left in the ruins, and the ever-present feeling of being watched.

The Architects' methods were far more sophisticated than they had initially anticipated. They weren't relying on brute force; they were manipulating time itself to their advantage. They seemed to anticipate their every move, creating obstacles and diversions to slow their progress and divert them from their goal. They were masters of deception, their actions deliberately calculated to destabilize and disorient the Chrononauts.

One such diversion was a seemingly harmless encounter with a group of nomadic tribespeople. At first, they seemed friendly and helpful, offering them guidance through the treacherous terrain. However, Anya quickly noticed inconsistencies in their clothing, their language, and their behavior – subtle anomalies that suggested their past and present were somehow intertwined.

Mason's temporal scanner confirmed her suspicions. The tribespeople weren't who they seemed; they were temporal anomalies, inadvertently manipulated by the Architects to mislead and distract the Chrononauts. It became clear that the Architects weren't just using brute force; they were employing a complex strategy of deception, deploying a range of temporal anomalies to hunt their prey, and throw them off their trail. The Architects' strategic deployment of temporal anomalies underscored the scale of their operation and the considerable resources they commanded.

The chase through the Siberian wilderness was a desperate race against time, a grueling test of endurance and resourcefulness. The Chrononauts had to rely on their combined skills – Mason's scientific expertise, Anya's strategic thinking, and Jacob's determination – to navigate the treacherous terrain and evade their relentless pursuers. The chase involved a perilous trek through the Siberian wilderness; overcoming blizzards, traversing frozen rivers and narrowly escaping crumbling ice sheets, all while evading the Architects' watchful eyes.

Finally, after weeks of relentless pursuit and perilous escapes, they found it - the rare earth element, nestled deep within the collapsed mine, emitting a faint luminescence even in the darkness. It was encased in a protective casing, shielding it from the temporal anomalies that plagued the area. But as they reached for it, a surge of temporal energy erupted from the mine's depths, revealing a hidden chamber.

Emerging from the shadows were several figures, clad in dark attire, their faces hidden by hooded masks – The Architects. Their leader, a tall, imposing figure, stepped forward, his voice echoing through the chamber. "The game is over," he declared, his voice chillingly calm. "The device will be ours."

The confrontation was inevitable. It was a fight not just for the device, but for the very fabric of time itself. The Architects, armed with their mastery of temporal mechanics, unleashed a barrage of temporal distortions, creating unpredictable shifts in time and space, attempting to disorient and overwhelm the Chrononauts. The battle raged on, a chaotic dance of temporal anomalies and desperate maneuvers, with the Chrononauts fighting to retain control and preserve the integrity of the timeline.

The fight was brutal and relentless, testing their limits, both physical and mental. They used their knowledge of temporal physics to counter the Architects' attacks, creating localized temporal shields to protect themselves from the worst of the distortions, and employed strategic maneuvers to exploit the unpredictable nature of the time-stream.

As the battle reached its climax, Jacob found himself facing the Architect's leader, the weight of his great-uncle's legacy bearing down on him. He knew this was their final chance, a desperate gamble to safeguard the future. He channeled his determination and courage to fight for the future, the fate of countless timelines resting on his shoulders. The struggle was intense, and each moment threatened to alter the fabric of reality.

The rare earth element pulsed with an eerie, inner light, a beacon in the suffocating darkness of the hidden chamber. It felt wrong, profoundly wrong, to simply take it. Jacob stared at it, his hand hovering inches away, the weight of centuries pressing down on him. This wasn't just a piece of metal; it was a potential key to reshaping history, a power that could unravel or rewrite the very fabric of existence. The Architects' leader, a chilling figure shrouded in shadow, watched him with predatory intensity. The air crackled with unspoken threats, with the weight of countless possibilities hanging in the balance.

The fight had been brutal, a chaotic ballet of temporal distortions and desperate maneuvers. Anya had used her wit and tactical prowess to counter the Architects' attacks, creating localized temporal shields to protect themselves from the worst of the temporal storms. Mason, ever the scientist, had tirelessly monitored their surroundings, his instruments beeping and whirring, frantically adjusting their temporal positioning to avoid being swept away into the unpredictable currents of time. But even their combined skill couldn't completely negate the Architects' control.

The encounter with the nomadic tribespeople, now revealed as temporal anomalies, had left a mark on Jacob. Their existence itself was a testament to the Architects' manipulation of time, a stark reminder of the ripple effects of altering the past. He'd seen glimpses of their altered realities, fleeting images of lives warped and twisted beyond recognition. The thought of inadvertently creating such suffering, of inflicting such pain on countless individuals, chilled him to the bone.

He recalled his great-uncle Elias's sacrifice, the weight of his desperate gamble against the Architects. Elias had risked everything to protect the timeline, to preserve the integrity of history. Now, Jacob faced a similar choice, but the stakes felt exponentially higher. Elias's actions, though heroic, had undoubtedly created unforeseen consequences, pushing Jacob and his team into this very situation. Was he destined to repeat the same mistakes, caught in an endless cycle of temporal warfare?

The ethical dilemmas gnawed at him. Taking the element meant completing the anti-temporal distortion device, a weapon capable of thwarting the Architects' plans. It meant potentially saving countless timelines from their malevolent designs. But it also meant the possibility of altering the past, of creating unforeseen consequences that could ripple through history, causing untold damage and suffering. The notion of such unintended consequences filled him with a profound sense of responsibility and a deep fear of failure.

He thought of the Tunguska event itself, the devastation it had wrought. Was it right to interfere, even if it meant preventing the Architects from using the device for their own twisted purposes? What if his intervention caused a more catastrophic event, something far worse than the Tunguska blast? The line between preserving the past and altering it felt impossibly thin, a tightrope walk above an abyss of unknown consequences.

Anya's voice, sharp and clear, broke through his turmoil. "Jacob, we need to decide. They won't wait forever."

He looked at her, her face etched with concern. He saw the same struggle reflected in Mason's eyes, a silent acknowledgment of the impossible choice they faced. He knew he couldn't afford to hesitate. The Architects were gaining ground, their temporal distortions growing stronger, their presence more menacing.

"What if there's another way?" he asked, more to himself than to his companions. "What if we can disable the device without altering the past? What if we can find a loophole, a weakness in their plan, without resorting to altering the established timeline?"

Mason, ever the pragmatist, shook his head. "The blueprints are clear. This element is essential. There's no alternative solution."

But Jacob refused to accept that. He felt a spark of determination ignite within him, a refusal to be bound by limitations. He had always admired his great-uncle's courage and ingenuity, and he felt a surge of his uncle's spirit inspiring him to find another solution. He studied the blueprint again, searching for any detail, any clue that might offer an alternative. He spent hours poring over the schematics, fueled by adrenaline and the weight of responsibility.

He suddenly noticed something, a small, almost imperceptible detail that had eluded everyone else. A faint notation, almost erased by time, mentioned a potential substitute element, an element with similar properties but far less volatile. It was a long shot, but it was a possibility, a pathway that might allow them to neutralize the device without altering the past.

"There's another option," he announced, pointing to the almost invisible notation. "An alternative element. It's a risk, but it might work."

A wave of relief washed over Anya and Mason. The possibility of a different approach, one that didn't involve directly manipulating the past, offered a glimmer of hope. They immediately started researching the alternative element, searching for any historical record of its existence and location.

Their research led them to a remote island in the Pacific, a location untouched by time and largely unexplored. The journey was fraught with peril, but the potential reward outweighed the risk. They were not only running from the Architects but against time itself, to find a solution that aligned with the ethical standards that guided their quest.

The search for the alternative element was a race against the Architects' relentless pursuit. They had to navigate treacherous terrain, overcome natural obstacles and evade the Architects' carefully planned traps. The island itself posed unique challenges. Its unique ecosystem, largely untouched by time, presented unique challenges. They had to understand its delicate balance and work to minimize their impact on the environment.

Finally, after days of searching, they located the element, hidden deep within a volcanic cave. It pulsed with a softer, gentler light than the element they found in Siberia, and it felt different, more harmonious with the flow of time. This element seemed to resonate with a natural harmony and peace, a stark contrast to the volatile energy of its Siberian counterpart.

Successfully extracting the element, they returned to their time, successfully completing the anti-temporal distortion device. However, this new solution presented a new ethical dilemma: Would using a different element affect the timeline in ways they couldn't predict? Would it alter the course of history in subtle, unforeseen ways? This newfound uncertainty challenged their initial moral compass. Despite the successful completion of the device and their escape from the Architects, the Chrononauts continued to grapple with the complexities and consequences of their actions, understanding that the ethical considerations would remain a constant companion on their journey through time. They knew the fight wasn't over. The Architects were still out there, and the challenges of protecting the timeline were far from concluded. Their journey had only just begun.

(To be continued....)

ABOUT THE AUTHOR

Keith Finley

An American author who was born in a small town in South Carolina. Keith was influenced into writing as a small boy, growing up during the space race, and moon landings. Also lived during the rise in Hollywood's science fiction movies, and super hero series, which developed his interest in writing science fiction. His first book "Rewind" An adventure in time travel a search for the truth, is the first book of a series of time travel fiction novels.

BOOKS BY THIS AUTHOR

Rewind An Adventure In Time Travel A Search For The Truth!

Book one (a search for the truth!)
Nasa has designed a time travel device used to explore and study climate change. Mason Anderson is the project manager for the project. The time travel device has been installed on Nasa's new space shuttle called "Prospector." The device unknown to the crew is not supposed to be used until flight number three. The crew of the prospector activates the time travel device during the first maiden flight. The time travel device takes the crew to 1963, a few days before President Kennedy visit to Dallas. The crew makes a decision to try and stop the assassination. Book one covers their trip and events during that time.

Rewind Book Two An Adventure In Time Travel, A Jouney To Deja Vu!

The beginning of book two introduces the second main character of the time travel series. Jacob Walker is an 18-year-old son of a local beekeeper located in the town of Mineral Springs. His family sends him on a trip to New York City to attend his great uncle's funeral, and witness the reading of the will. On his trip to New York City, he gets ready to take his first subway ride. Unknown to Jacob, Mason Anderson is also in New York, he has found the time travel device, and is currently running from Nasa agents. Nasa has discovered the unknown secret that the device can travel to a specific time in history, which they want to use to alter history. Mason doesn't want Nasa to use his device in such a way so he takes the device and is running from Nasa. Book two covers their trip, and events which leads to them joining forces and take them on their next time travel adventure in book three.